USA TODAY BESTSELLING AUTHOR
Dale Mayer

NIKOLAI 06
SHADOW RECON

NIKOLAI: SHADOW RECON, BOOK 6
Beverly Dale Mayer
Valley Publishing Ltd.

Copyright © 2023

All rights reserved. Except for use in any review, the reproduction or utilization of this work in whole or in part by any electronic, mechanical or other means, now known or hereafter invented, including xerography, photocopying and recording, or in any information storage or retrieval system, is forbidden without the written permission of the publisher.

This is a work of fiction. Names, characters, places, brands, media, and incidents are either the product of the author's imagination or are used fictitiously. Any resemblance to actual events, locales, or persons, living or dead, is entirely coincidental.

ISBN-13: 978-1-773367-37-8
Print Edition

Books in This Series

Magnus, Book 1
Rogan, Book 2
Egan, Book 3
Barret, Book 4
Whalen, Book 5
Nikolai, Book 6
Teegan, Book 7

About This Book

Deep in the permafrost of the Arctic, a joint task force, comprised of over one dozen countries, comes together to level up their winter skills. A mix of personalities, nationalities, and egos bring out the best—and the worst—as these globally elite men and women work and play together. They rub elbows with hardy locals and a group of scientists gathered close by …

One fatality is almost expected with this training. A second is tough but not a surprise. However, when a third goes missing? It's hard to not be suspicious. When the missing man is connected to one of the elite Maverick team members and is a special friend of Lieutenant Commander Mason Callister? All hell breaks loose …

Nikolai had been at the camp almost since the beginning. His friend had been one of the first to go missing. Although he'd had more specialist arctic training than anyone else in the camp, something had still gone wrong. He can't understand what could have happened and as they slowly find out more bits and pieces, he realizes the hidden connection his friend had withheld from him all these years…

Emily wasn't going to say no to Mason, but his request wasn't along her normal line of duties. Still given the circumstances, she could understand him asking. Although answers were a little thin on the ground particularly when another body shows and shocks them all.

When is enough enough? What does the person behind this mess want? What is his end game? With Nikolai at her side, they need to find out... before someone decides that Nikolai knows more than he's telling...

Sign up to be notified of all Dale's releases here!

https://geni.us/DaleNews

PROLOGUE

NIKOLAI STARED DOWN at the man he'd called a friend for many a year, a man he had already grieved as lost out in the winter wonderland, but one who he'd hoped against hope had survived somehow. And to see his body now laid out in front of him in this state—having been shot by the woman his friend had attacked in the middle of the night in the very military training center the shooter had forsaken for whatever dumb-ass reason—was completely beyond Nikolai's understanding.

He didn't even know what to say, yet he knew that this dead man was immediately under suspicion by everybody else. But Nikolai didn't know anything and certainly had no explanation for the actions of his friend. He couldn't even begin to believe that his "friend" had done this.

He looked over at the others and declared, "It's him, no doubt about that, but, before you ask me a million questions..." He paused, shaking his head. "I don't know why he's done whatever he's done. I don't know where he's been or how's he's been getting by since he disappeared. I don't even know why he would have left in the first place," he explained. "I don't really know how he could possibly have been fine out there all this time." Then he stopped and added, "Well, that part I probably could answer, at least to some degree. His family, his uncle, was from Siberia. If anybody would have winter survival skills, it would be him."

"So why was he here then?" Magnus asked. "Why come for this training?"

"I think he wanted to see if you all had any other skills he didn't know about. He used to laugh about it," Nikolai shared reluctantly.

"And yet, you are part of the Russian team, so you ought to have the same skill set."

"No, that's incorrect," Nikolai stated flatly. "I'm not part of the Russian team. I'm part of the Swiss team. Just like you have people from other countries here on your US team, I am from the Swiss team," he repeated. "My family moved to Switzerland when I was very young," he shared, as he looked back to the body of his supposed friend. "This guy," he pointed to the cold dead corpse, "wasn't even part of the Russian team. I don't ... He came over on a special assignment for Russia, but he was talking about leaving, about finding a way to switch his team somehow. He wanted to be somewhere else, but I don't know that he ever did anything about it. The thing about him was that he was all talk. He had lots of plans, big plans. I... I've done actual missions with him. I've been on bases worldwide with him too. But never have I seen him do anything even remotely like he's done this time."

"And yet you would have considered him a friend?" Magnus asked.

"Yeah, well, apparently I don't know what that means anymore," Nikolai stated bitterly. He looked over to see Emily, one of the few women on the base, standing and staring at him. He looked at her and frowned. "Honestly, I don't know anything about this," he said to the men, not wanting this discussion to be out in the open.

Yet Emily wasn't moving. He turned to her and asked, "Don't you have someplace to be?"

"No, I don't," she snapped. "I think, at this point in time, anything that is happening in the training base needs to be something the rest of us get to hear about. Instead of us finding out through the grapevine afterward," she said, shooting Magnus a look, which spoke volumes about the confidence she had in all of them telling the truth.

Magnus stared at her for a moment and didn't say anything, then he turned back to Nikolai. "So, Nikolai, what can you tell me about him? Anything more?"

"Not really, outside of the fact that he came over on the Russian team and wanted to shift to another country. And, yeah, I'd thought we were friends, but I obviously can't tell you much more than that."

"Is he married? Does he have family? Would he have been coerced into doing something like this?"

"No, he would have thought it was a lark," Nikolai declared flatly. "He always thought he was better than everybody else around him. He always knew that he was very, very good at winter survival skills, and he knew that he could live out here way easier than anybody else. Honestly he spent complete winters outside with his grandfather. This Arctic tundra is not a hardship for him because he knew how to survive out there."

"And you didn't think to tell anybody that?" Magnus asked.

"Tell them what? He disappeared. Besides, all that he could do and all that he was must be in his file. I didn't know what had happened to him. After being missing all this time, I assumed he probably died out there. We just didn't know how or why," he noted. "And, for that, I'm sorry because, if he needed my help, I presumed he would have asked for it, and, since he didn't, I have to presume he had plans all on his own."

"And yet, if he wanted to move to another country, such as to the US or somewhere else, this is hardly the place to do it."

"I know. I know, and he talked a lot about that, but I don't know if he ever would have gone." He looked over to Emily again, still staring at him, a hard look on her face. He frowned. "You don't need to be here. This is my private business."

"A man is dead," she stated. "It is no longer your private business."

He flushed, realizing that she wouldn't back down, and that none of the men here seemed to want to help him in that regard. "I don't have anything else to tell you. I don't know what happened. It doesn't look good for him, and I guess in your minds it doesn't look good for me," he stated, as he shook his head. "But I didn't have anything to do with this, and I don't see how you can possibly blame me for something that he's done."

"We aren't blaming you," Emily said immediately. "So take the chip off your shoulder already."

He glared at her. "A little hard to do when everybody's staring at me, as if this is something I'm involved in. I don't know what he was up to. He was my friend, but he was also an arrogant know-it-all, and, if he thought this would be something he could do to mess up everything here, he would do it," Nikolai stated, then raised both hands. "And, right about now, I want to kill him myself, but somebody else apparently already got the job done."

"It was a fair and justified shooting," Magnus replied.

Nikolai nodded, with a shrug. "I know that. I'm sorry, and I didn't mean to imply anything differently. This has been quite a shock for me too." And, with that, he added, "I'll go get a cup of coffee and find a place to sit and think about what this means—and mourn the friend I used to know—because it sure as hell couldn't have been the same guy who did this."

And, with that, he turned and, daring anybody to stop him, walked away.

DAY 1 EVENING

NIKOLAI KERSAF DIDN'T even know where to go or what to do. He stood outside, bundled up, and he had a craving worse than he ever had before. He wanted to smoke so bad, but he'd quit years ago. So even the fact that he wanted one right now revealed his elevated stress—which needed to dissipate because it wouldn't get any easier, at least not for a while. When the door burst open behind him, he stiffened. When he heard a woman's voice behind him, he wasn't surprised to find Emily Deshawn. "I'm fine," he muttered, with a wave of his hand. "Go back inside."

"You say that, but you've received a major shock and want to be alone to deal with it. Yet this is not the place to do that."

"Really? And who made you the expert here?"

"Nobody, but I learned from watching other people in this base die from the same foolhardy, egotistical attitude of always being right."

Startled, he looked over at her. "I'm not egotistical, and I'm sure as hell not any of those other things you're thinking, and I'm especially not suicidal," he snapped. "So, you can get that idea right out of your head."

"I'd love to," she declared in a clipped tone, but her gaze was searching, as she studied his features, making him that much more aware of her and their surroundings. Her cheeks were quickly turning bright pink, and she was slapping her hands together to try to stay warm.

He motioned at her body. "You'll freeze to death if you don't go back inside."

"I won't," she argued, "at least not while I try to coerce you back into the building." She had a forced smile on her face. "Look. I know you lost a friend, and you're bound to be really upset right now."

"More than a friend and more than a loss," he bit off. "It's a betrayal. It's a lot of things that I'm still trying to figure out, and I don't know how to pigeonhole it yet. I'm out here trying to think, and I do that best alone," he stated pointedly.

"I get it," she noted, with a half smile, "but that doesn't mean you'll get that option right now. If you don't want to hear it from me, one of the others will tell you the same thing." She shook her head, as she motioned at the door behind her. "I volunteered."

"Why would you do that? It's obvious you don't like me."

She looked at him, startled. "Doesn't matter whether I like you or not," she noted, turning pale right before his eyes. "I don't want to see you dead. And, besides, how would you know if I like you or not?" she asked, with a snort. "You've ignored me."

"Yeah, I was leaving you and your girlfriend alone," he explained, with a wave of his hand. "I thought you might want some privacy here, since there isn't much to be had."

Her gaze was equally startled, as his had been when she stared at him. "Girlfriend?" she repeated. "I hope you mean that in a platonic way."

Confused, he frowned at her. "I thought you guys were

partners."

"No, we're not, and, if we were, I sure as hell wouldn't make it public on a military base," she muttered. "Talk about suicidal."

He shrugged. "Some countries are more liberal in their views," he said. "I certainly am."

"That's nice," she agreed, with a smirk. "Alicia and I have been friends for a very long time, and, with all the shit going on, we're keeping a close eye on each other. She is seeing somebody here," she shared, with a smile. "I'm facilitating their privacy."

"Good for you," he conceded. "Little enough of that for any of us."

"True enough, and you're not getting it right now either, no matter how much you snap at me."

Her blunt response startled a laugh out of him, and he smiled.

"See? That's not so hard."

"Says you," he muttered. "Nothing is easy about any of this. If I had had some idea where Eric had been all this time, I would probably feel a bit better."

"I think we all would," she confirmed. "With all the other deaths, and still one missing—unless you count Amelia too—then I'm sure that everybody is wondering whether he's really missing or not."

"*Teegan*," Nikolai noted. "I knew him too, even a little before he joined the military, then rarely after that. However, once in a while, we would cross paths, but not very often. We were both doing a scuba diving training course a while back and really hit it off then. He told me how he was coming here, and I was happy to spend some time with him. Then he disappeared too."

"Any idea if your friend Teegan would have had a hand in helping Eric go missing—or vice versa?"

He frowned at her, startled, then shook his head. "God, I hope not. However, if you're asking me if I know for sure, then, no, of course not. Not now," he shared, raising his hands in frustration. "We're all confused over what's going on. … I would have thought they were both dead, since so much time has gone by. The fact that one of them, Eric, was alive until last night, means he had some place to hole up, while the rest of us risked our lives out there looking for him. It pisses me off to no end, but I don't have any answers for you."

"How about helping me find some then?"

He stared at her. "What do you mean, help you find some?" he asked curiously. "Why you?"

"It'll be all of us obviously, but Teegan was a friend of mine too. And I had walked away from any thought that he could possibly still be alive, so now I feel as if I shortchanged him," she admitted. "I want to help—if by any chance he is alive. Get him home safely."

"Why ask me to help?"

"Because you have a reason to sort it out," she admitted, with an awkward glance in his direction. "You have a reason to get answers. Yet maybe you don't care, or maybe this Eric guy pissed you off enough that you were okay when he disappeared." He glared at her, and she shrugged. "The shit we've heard since we've been here has been pretty wild, so any number of reasons could exist as to why you wouldn't want to help me."

"For one thing, it's dangerous," he snapped. "I don't even know what skills you have or if you're really serious." That clarified what he thought of her.

"I'm serious," she said. "Everybody will be trying to figure it out. So, if you help us, I'm pretty sure that people would at least take you at your word and accept that you're not involved."

"Wow." He gave her a forced smile. "I really don't give a shit what other people think."

"Maybe you should," she replied. "At least right now, when everybody is trying to decide whose side you're on." He stared at her in shock. She shrugged. "Think about it. Eric was your friend, your buddy, and you probably knew the most about him. Yet, even though he was heavily skilled in winter survival to the point that, for him, it wasn't even a skill but a natural part of breathing, you didn't say anything about it. That makes everybody suspicious."

"There really wasn't anything to say," he snapped, wondering at the frustration rising inside him. "I told a bunch of people. I even told Joe one time, when I was out visiting him and the dogs. I also told Yegorahn… but he's dead now. I told …"

Nikolai frowned, as he pondered the others who he had shared this info with. "I told the rest of Eric's Russian team and mine—the Swiss team. I mean, everybody at the training exercises knew that Eric was quite adept at surviving in winter conditions. However, after so many weeks supposedly missing out here, you don't think anybody would have survived because there were no signs, no signals."

Nikolai continued. "The Arctic weather here is all too much, and I had my doubts. It's not a case of me holding back information. It's more that I didn't keep reiterating it because I didn't have any hope that Eric was still out there," he explained, his tone turning flat. "What is it you think you'll do that nobody else is already doing?"

"I don't know that I can do anything more than the others," she admitted, "but I don't want to lose sight of the fact that, if Eric survived… maybe Teegan could too."

"I suppose you're sweet on Teegan then?" He hoped she didn't notice the odd tone in his voice.

"No, not at all," she confirmed, with a snort. "However, I'm very fond of the living, and it seems as if we're up against challenges here that none of us expected. It's one thing to be up against the elements, and, in a worst-case scenario, you expect certain things when you're against that enemy." She took in a deep breath to add, "But this? … This is something I don't recognize." Then her voice dropped as she admitted, "And I don't like it."

His heart lurched slightly, as he nodded. "Yeah, you and me both. This is something none of us expected, and, for me, this is a betrayal at a level I hadn't really thought possible."

"And yet," she noted, with a slight nod in his direction, "when you get over that shock, it's almost as if you don't know what to do in order to make this okay."

"What if there isn't any *making it okay*? Did you think about that?"

"I think we're all thinking about that to some degree because what if this Eric guy was responsible for a whole lot of the other hell we've all been going through?"

"Do you think I'm not thinking that too?" he snapped, glaring at her again.

She smiled. "Hold the temper a little bit," she murmured. "Like it or not, we are all on the same team here, so let's try to think of this a little more calmly."

He groaned. "I've been standing out here, trying to figure out why Eric wouldn't have told me what he was after, what he was doing, but none of it makes any sense," he shared, with obvious frustration.

Then the door behind them opened, and Mountain stepped out, looking positively ferocious. He glared at the two of them and barked, "Both of you get your butts back inside, right now!"

She looked over at Nikolai and said, "Come on. Let's go."

And, with that, although reluctantly, Nikolai allowed himself to be pushed back into the building. As he walked past Mountain, he muttered in a frustrated tone, "You could always ask nicely."

"If you weren't out there being a dumbass," Mountain snapped, "I would have." And, with that, Mountain nudged him inside and pulled the door closed behind them. "Obviously we all have to rethink what's happened, and we all should have a conversation and sort it out."

"Oh, and here I thought Emily would do it all on her own." Nikolai smirked.

Mountain shot her a look.

She shrugged. "I will delve into this," she declared. "Teegan was a friend of mine, and I have no intention of giving up on him, especially now that there's a real chance that he's still alive."

Mountain nodded slowly, his jaw ticking. "This has given us all a new sense of urgency in trying to solve this. None of us wanted to believe Teegan had gone under in the first place, and now we have reason to believe that maybe something else entirely is happening."

Nikolai shook his head. "And yet we can't be acting like idiots," he noted harshly. "I don't know what happened to Teegan, and I don't know what happened to Eric," he added, with a sigh and a shake of his head. "Believe me. I wish I'd had the chance to get my hands on Eric while the man was still alive, so I could shake some answers out of him," he growled.

"As if that's an option …" Emily grunted.

"It's not an option in that sense," Mountain replied, "but that doesn't mean it isn't something that we need to do regardless."

Nikolai frowned at him and asked, "You mean, in terms of backtracking where he was, how he got here, and what he was doing?"

"Exactly."

Emily nodded, looking to both of them.

"Maybe one of the first things we need to look at is whether Eric ever left," Nikolai suggested, as if he were thinking out loud to himself, more than to any of them.

At that, Mountain studied him, then slowly nodded. "*Huh*, that's worth a hard look. We're having a confab in ten minutes in the dining room." He looked to both of them. "We want you there. Both of you."

"Is this an interrogation or an invitation to cross-check information and see what we can solve?" Nikolai asked.

"It's an invitation to help," Mountain clarified. "Teegan is my brother. Regardless of whatever you think is happening here, I want him home."

And, with that, Mountain stomped away.

⊕

EMILY TURNED AND looked at Nikolai. "I didn't know that they were brothers, did you?"

Nikolai shrugged. "I'd heard rumors."

She stared at the mountain of a man, as he strolled away. "Christ, that's got to be hard. I wonder if that's why he came up."

"Sure, but, jeez, he's been here for weeks, and still we have more questions than answers. Where was Eric staying? What was he even doing?"

"Better yet, how was he surviving out there?" she muttered.

"I don't know." He looked over at her. "Are you part of the meetings?"

She shook her head. "Not before this."

"Mountain's right. We need to use all our resources, pull our information together, and figure out what the hell's going on."

"I'm also a little concerned about something else."

"What's that?" he asked, looking at her, as they walked toward the kitchen.

"I don't think Eric could have done all this mischief alone." As they entered the dining room, her words carried across the room to the group of men sitting at one of the big tables. Including the new investigator, Samson, she'd heard about but hadn't spoken to yet. She was wary of his intense gaze as she sat down.

Magnus looked at her and nodded. "Agreed."

She frowned at him, and he frowned right back.

Emily shrugged. "It's really too much chaos for Eric to have managed on his own all this time. ... Isn't it? If this was warfare, then maybe not, but these conditions, this climate, is all something he is quite comfortable with. What I don't understand is why though. What was he ultimately after, and did he have anything to do with these other missing persons, accidents, deaths, and other problems around here?"

"That's what we'll have to figure out," Magnus agreed. He motioned behind them, as Mountain came in. "Also one of Mountain's questions."

Mountain eyed her, one eyebrow raised. "As to whether Eric's worked alone?"

"Yes," she confirmed. "I can't see that all this—"

Magnus pointed at the chairs. "Sit down."

DAY 1 LATE EVENING

EMILY IMMEDIATELY SAT down. She wasn't sure who these men were, but she was pretty sure they all knew each other and were all here for the same reason. She'd heard everybody else talking and whispering about them, but nobody ever came out and said anything.

Every stranger was treated with suspicion. People stuck close to their own teams, their own groups, and friends they had made, in the hopes that whatever bad juju running rampant through the base would skip them. The last thing anybody wanted was to get caught in this maelstrom of negative events.

Emily glanced at the coffeepot but decided to ignore it. So when Nikolai brought her a cup and placed it in front of her, she was surprised. "Thank you."

He nodded. "You'll need it after being outside that long."

She shrugged. "Could have come in earlier." He glared at her, but she smiled and patted the seat beside her. "Sit and take a load off your mind."

At that, the other men snorted, and Nikolai gave a half laugh. "You do have an attitude."

"I do," she agreed, with a smile. "Also I want to see progress happening here."

"And yet," Magnus replied, with a pointed look in her

direction, "we've got a shot at seeing some progress now."

"How sad that it requires yet another dead body for that to happen," she added.

Magnus nodded. "Oh, I agree, but in this case? ... I don't want to say it's the right body, but it's someone we didn't expect, and it opens other avenues that we hadn't really speculated about," Magnus noted. "So, a lot we need to consider."

"How many here think that Eric's got to be working with somebody?" Emily asked, as she watched their gazes shift among each other.

"I don't know if he *has* to be working with somebody," Mountain clarified cautiously. "However, I would suspect that, whatever he was doing, it would definitely be easier with somebody helping. However, if he was as egotistical, proud, and ornery as Nikolai here seems to think Eric was, then I can see him doing it solo because he could. And then maybe standing back and enjoying a laugh at our expense."

Nikolai immediately nodded. "That's exactly who he was. Eric would stand in the darkness and watch everybody else struggle and think nothing of it," he shared.

"Wow." Emily frowned at Nikolai. "I didn't have a chance to even get to know this guy, but now I'm grateful that I didn't because he sounds like an absolute ass."

"He was in many ways," Nikolai confirmed, "and he didn't make friends easily. He was a loner mostly because he was too good. He was one of those guys who was good at everything, and he knew it. He often would make other people feel uncomfortable, inferior even, because it seemed that everything was so easy for him," Nikolai shook his head. "Too easy."

"So, he was kind of a jack of all trades?" Magnus asked.

"More or less. It didn't matter what field it was, but he would excel, and, in that excelling, he was always laughing at everybody else who struggled. It didn't matter whether mechanics, electronics, war games, shooting." Nikolai glanced around at the men. "It didn't matter. He was very good at all of it."

"However, living out on the tundra is hard long-term excelling," Magnus noted. "Nobody can be perfect all the time."

"And yet," Nikolai replied, "I've never really seen Eric fail, which is another reason this surprises me. Ultimately he failed this time, but I don't understand what would make him try to do this in the first place. Whatever 'this' is."

"Obviously Eric thought either Chrissy knew something or he needed to stop her from finding something, so he was intent on killing her. However, the fact that we now have him in our makeshift morgue changes everything," Mountain noted, as he shifted in his seat, making it creak beside them.

When Emily looked at the chair in alarm, his gaze shot in her direction. He shrugged. "I don't break chairs very often, and, if I do, they weren't that well built in the first place."

"Maybe so." She winced. "But when you go down, you'll go hard."

"Yeah, the bigger we are, the harder we fall," he stated. "But I've been there before, so it's really not an issue, so let's get back to the subject at hand. All I have in my notes is that everything was normal on Eric's last day here. Plenty of people saw him. He was outside while we were doing war games that day. Two teams, everybody against each other, and nobody had live rounds. It was a training exercise, one full of camaraderie and fun, yet Eric never came back in that day, correct?"

"That's correct," Nikolai confirmed. "Eric hadn't really wanted to go out and do the games either. He thought them foolish and felt he was above such things. He wanted to go out with live rounds and told me, if people were any good, then they wouldn't get shot."

At that, Magnus looked at him with one eyebrow raised. "So, he was that kind of a maverick, was he?"

"Yes," Nikolai agreed. "He didn't have a whole lot of respect for others, as you can tell."

"Got it. So did he have any other friends here?"

"Not that I would have called his friends. He was friendly enough to other people here, but I'm not sure how many people really understood who Eric was on the inside though."

"Did he ever get violent with you?" Emily asked. When he frowned at her, she shrugged. "The guy reappeared here just to attack Chrissy and Whalen—twice. Did you ever see that level of violence?"

"*Umm.*" Nikolai stopped and frowned.

"Obviously that question took a little more thinking," she noted calmly, looking straight at him. "What is it that you're trying not to say?"

"It's not that I'm trying *not* to say it. I'm trying to put into words something that I hadn't really considered."

"How about spitting it out," Mountain declared. "We really don't have time for more than that."

Nikolai glared at him. "For you guys, this is easy. However, as flawed as Eric was, this was a friend of mine."

"I'm not sure he's a friend as much as he might have used you to help him fit in," Emily suggested.

Nikolai frowned, then surprisingly slowly nodded. "And that is something he would do."

"Was he socially awkward or something? Because I sure don't remember seeing that side of him," Emily noted.

"Not at all. He always seemed to have a group of people around him, almost as if he developed fan clubs easily. People either really loved him or really hated him, but he generally had more fans than enemies, if that makes sense."

"It does." Magnus nodded. "I've seen people like that before too. But here is the real question. Does any of that help us?"

"I think it does," Nikolai stated. "If Eric was trying to set up something, he wouldn't have had any trouble getting people to do his bidding."

"You mean to help him?" Mountain asked.

"Yes," Nikolai agreed. "And Eric would have done it in such a way that they would have thought it a lark or a game, or that he had some top-secret clearance, or that he was the chosen one to do a special mission. And, if he had done something such as that, I don't know that anybody would have jumped to participate because the consequences would have been pretty rough, and Eric wouldn't be around to back them up."

"Right," Emily noted. "So you're saying that, if somebody got caught in Eric's web of magical lies, they wouldn't have told anybody?"

"I don't think so," Nikolai murmured. "He was really a specialist in this kind of winter survival living, and yet it didn't occur to me to ask why he'd bothered to come. Everybody here came to learn, and Eric had already done it all."

"So why was he even here?" Emily asked.

At that, Nikolai looked at Emily with raised eyebrows. "On a special assignment. And if this was something he had planned, who would he plan it with? How would he plan it? And more so, why would he have come in the first place, unless to implement this plan somehow?"

"What plan though?" Magnus asked, looking at Mountain. "What was his plan? Eric attacked Chrissy and Whalen in the middle of the night, but why?"

Mountain shrugged. "Because Eric thought Chrissy knew something. What went wrong in Eric's world that he would go this pathway to begin with?"

At that, all of them turned to look at Nikolai. "I don't know, and, no, he never did drugs, if that's the question. He thought drugs were nasty, inferior, and made you do things you didn't want to do. He believed control was everything. Eric was… he was both a man's man and a ladies' man. The women loved him because he was really macho, even arrogant, but in a way that they seemed to love." Nikolai shrugged. "Not sure how that works, but the men also really liked Eric. He had that … *charisma*, I guess you would call it. I think that's why everybody was so stunned when he disappeared because, from their perspective, he could do everything. Yet, when it seemed he'd been caught out there and had presumably died, they didn't know what they were supposed to think about him anymore because it didn't gel with the image they had of him."

The conversation died at that point in time, and Emily turned and looked around the dining room, then whispered to Magnus, "Will you tell everyone about Eric?"

He nodded. "Yes, but we'll do it in a meeting in the morning, where we can watch the reactions."

She frowned at him. "In case somebody here is involved?"

"Of course," he stated. "Wouldn't you?"

"Sure," she said, "absolutely I would. And, if someone was involved at this point, when things have gotten so bad and so deep, I'm not sure how far they might go in order to hide that."

"Depends on what level of involvement it may have been," Nikolai noted. "If we find any implication that they had something to do with these deaths, they'll do a lot to hide that from us. Nobody wants to go to jail, especially a military court, over the death of other military personnel," he pointed out.

"Which makes whoever else is here, had plotted with Eric, protected him, or sheltered him, as dangerous as a rattlesnake," she muttered.

"I don't know about a rattlesnake," Magnus interjected, "but you can bet that they'll fight for their life now because this is what it's come to. What they're prepared to hide is something we don't quite understand because we don't know how far they've gone. Neither do we understand what they're trying to keep us from learning, assuming that they're even here."

"A big frozen tundra is out there," Nikolai noted, "and, although most people don't like or appreciate that world, it doesn't change the fact that a whole lot of other people live quite happily here."

"You're talking about the village of locals?" Samson spoke for the first time.

"Yes," Nikolai replied, "I'm talking about the village, what some call the Inuit settlement, plus the scientists' camp."

"So, back to Amelia," Mountain stated, with a nod, and

silence came.

"Are we really thinking Amelia might have helped Eric?" Emily asked.

"I don't know who might have helped him," Mountain admitted, "but I can tell you that somebody likely did. Eric's been on his own for weeks now. He would need a lot of supplies out in the middle of nowhere."

Samson frowned. "Sure, but, from what Nikolai's shared, Eric's probably been able to hunt, and he's probably been fine on simple rations because it's something he's used to. He might even have reveled in it, him against the world—or him against the base. Maybe he was doing it more as a lark to ensure nobody could find him. Maybe he was happy to prove that he had that power over everybody, knowing that he was capable of staying hidden and that they were useless, helpless, when it came to finding him," Samson suggested.

"That would be very much like him," Nikolai confirmed, with a nod.

Emily frowned. "But what then? Did it turn around sideways on him—so he's the one getting hurt by it—or does he go crazy?"

At that, the men turned toward her.

She shrugged. "You and I both know that can happen. Think about it. He's alone in the world, too isolated, struggling, knowing that a group here is all tucked in and warm, and he walked away from it as a joke. However, now it's become something he can't laugh about anymore, so it becomes an anger, a burning hatred inside him, all against this base," she pointed out. "I can see it, even if you guys can't." She pivoted to Nikolai. "Could you see that being him too?"

Nikolai frowned, his fingers tapping on the tabletop, his lips twisting as he pondered her words. "If people didn't play the game the way Eric thought they should, he could get very irritated, angry at their lack of skill, their failure to grasp his intention, and even at their varied perspectives."

"So, a control freak through and through," Mountain suggested.

Nikolai nodded. "I guess that's a better way to put it. A very short fuse when it came to people's inherent stupidity. So, building on Emily's scenario, if Eric was thinking, in his mind, that this game was supposed to go in another direction or that we should have found him by now—and he can't come back in until he's found—then, yes, in a way, I could see him going off the deep end," Nikolai murmured. "Maybe, after all this time, he did go a little nuts."

"But why kill the way he did? Why not come in and take everybody out?"

"You mean, by fire or carbon monoxide poisoning?" he asked pointedly. "We've had two fires here that I know of and some generator issues and, of course, the attempt on the scientists' camp."

Mountain asked, "Would Eric have had anything to do with the attacks at the village?" At that, everybody stiffened and turned to look at Mountain. This was obviously news to everyone around the table.

"Attacks at the village?" Emily asked in shock.

He nodded. "Yes, in the middle of the night and anonymous. They have no idea who has been slowly attacking the village, taking foodstuffs, hurting a couple elders, not killing anyone yet, taking fresh kills, things such as that," he shared.

"But those are the signs of a man who's looking to survive out here and doesn't want to be found," Emily stated in a hoarse whisper.

"Exactly," Mountain agreed, "so you have to consider who could be in that position. If someone was trying to survive out there and wanted to be found and commended on his skills, then no need for these kind of shenanigans."

"Shit," she muttered. "I don't even want to think about that."

"I feel bad for the villagers as it is," Magnus stated. "They must really think that we're absolutely nuts if we can't control our own people. They know we've had missing people, killings, not to mention all the bizarre accidents."

DAY 2 WEE MORNING HOURS

BY THE TIME the meeting was over, a matter of hours before breakfast, Emily's mind floated in circles at the horrible options. The news that the village had been attacked several times was troublesome. That some of the elders had been hurt bothered her more than she could imagine, as she headed back to her room slowly, her arms wrapped around her chest.

She wondered if she could get any sleep, when Nikolai called out to her. She turned and watched as he strode to her. "Hey," she greeted him.

"You okay?" Nikolai asked her.

She nodded. "Tired." Even as she said it, she yawned.

"Go get some sleep," he murmured. "We'll talk later this morning." And, with that, he headed toward his room.

She watched him go and noted he was only a couple doors away from her.

Before he went in, he turned and smiled at her. "Thanks for coming out and looking after me tonight." He went inside and closed the door.

She was surprised but pleased at his attitude shift. It wasn't long before she was in bed and crashed.

LATER THAT MORNING, Nikolai sat back in the general assembly meeting of all on base, deliberately trying to keep an eye on everybody as they heard the news. There were moments of complete shock, followed by a flurry of questions, as everybody wanted answers as to where Eric had been, what he'd been doing, why he'd come in, and it went on and on.

Finally Magnus lifted a hand and cut off the ruckus. "Look," he called out in a raised voice. "We don't have all the answers, but we're working on it. If anybody knows anything about Eric's last few hours, days, weeks while he was here, anybody who was friends with him, anybody who knew anything about him... please contact us."

One of the men seated at the front shouted, "That would be Nikolai."

"Nikolai has already come forward. However, we need to hear anything and everything. One way or another, we'll be talking to everybody on this base."

"Turning everything upside hasn't done a damn bit of good any other time, has it?" asked one of the men in a surly tone.

"Look at how many people are dead," added another one, "but maybe now we can find out why and who might be behind some of it."

"Do you really think Eric was behind any of those deaths?" asked one of the other men, who stiffened and straightened up, glaring at everyone. "Obviously something got to him, or he was injected with drugs or something."

Nikolai stared at the man. He thought his name was Spencer, though he wasn't sure, but he was acting the way people around Eric often acted. As if Eric could walk on water and could do no wrong.

Magnus apparently had picked up on it too. "Obviously you knew him well enough," he began, "so why don't you tell me about him."

"Sure, I knew him. He was a good guy, a great guy," he declared, a bit too proud, as if he were honored knowing him. "He could do damn-near anything. That's why I know he wouldn't have done this. I don't know what the hell that story is about him attacking Chrissy and Whalen because that's not the kind of guy he was."

"When you say that's not the guy he was, what kind of guy was he?" Magnus asked immediately.

"Hey, give him a puzzle, and he could sort it out in five minutes. Give him a dismantled gun, he'd put it together in seconds. Give him a target ridiculously far away and a nearly impossible shot. He'd hit it, or, if he didn't hit it quite right the first time, he'd make damn sure he hit it the second or third time … or die trying," he stated. "He was driven, but he was a good guy. So I don't know what the hell is going on here or how whatever he was doing may have been misinterpreted, but he wouldn't have tried to hurt Chrissy."

"Interesting," Magnus replied. "Okay, we'll talk more in a few minutes." He looked around at the rest of the room. "Anybody else?"

Then the colonel walked in, and everybody stood at attention and saluted. He waved his hand and ordered, "At ease, soldiers." He looked over at Magnus. "My room in five minutes."

Magnus immediately nodded, and, as soon as the CO left, everybody relaxed. Magnus looked over at Nikolai. "This might require you too."

His eyebrows shot up. "I don't think he wants anything to do with me."

"You might be surprised." Magnus smiled. "Things aren't always as they seem."

"Yeah, you're not kidding," Nikolai said, scrunching his face. "I'm starting to realize that we can't seem to keep anything straight and clear here."

And, with that, Magnus disappeared as he headed down the hallway toward a meeting with the colonel.

Nikolai looked around to see Emily watching him. He stood and walked over, hearing the low chatter break out among the whole group, but mostly all were shocked at what they had heard.

She smiled, stood, and walked a few steps closer to Nikolai. "Notice anything?"

He shook his head and shrugged. "Nothing really."

"Right? Fun stuff," she muttered.

"Not really." He gave a half laugh, as he looked around. People were staring at him, but they were trying to not be obvious. He groaned. "I'll be a leper here for a while."

"Only until people figure out what's going on and remember that you were friends with Eric, but that doesn't mean that you were responsible for him."

"No, sure feels like it though," Nikolai mumbled. "I wish to God I had spoken up more."

"I'm sure you do, but, if you don't think anything is wrong, then you don't realize what you need to say."

"Eric's always been that guy Spencer described," Nikolai noted. "The one who could do everything. So, when he couldn't do everything and didn't come back that day, it was kind of a shock. Then you realize that Eric's glory days had run to an end, and he was human after all. And yet, I guess, the fact that we hadn't found his body was always in the back of my mind as being wrong. It nagged me as being a problem that we needed to do something about, but we searched time and time again and found nothing."

"Of course the weather here has hardly been conducive to finding anything or anyone," she pointed out. "We've had storm after storm after storm, and, within hours, all tracks were wiped out. It's not as if we haven't tried to find the missing men," she noted earnestly. "I've been out on search parties looking for him—and for Teegan and Amelia as well. We haven't found anything to lead us to any of these missing people."

"The Teegan situation gets to me too," Nikolai muttered.

"Hey, that gets to us all," she murmured. "He was much younger than a lot of them here, but he was friendly in a way that Eric wasn't. Your friend was more arrogant, whereas Teegan was fun and full of life."

"And yet, according to the rumors I'd heard, Teegan had some idea of wrongdoing here at the base and was likely taken out because of it."

"I heard those rumors too," she said, "and we should ask Magnus and Mountain about that now, rather than jumping to any conclusions."

"Wouldn't that be nice?" he quipped, with a half laugh.

She shrugged. "I would much prefer going to the source. Misinformation runs rampant in this place because everybody's on a need-to-know basis. Since we apparently didn't need to know, we've only now found out the hard way that this is an issue. All of a sudden, people want to know what we know. In this instance," she pointed out, "we are at a disadvantage because of that need-to-know ruling. Not that we can help out much, but still, it's a problem."

"And that's the thing because we do understand *need to*

know and why that's a thing, and generally we really don't need to know."

"I sure won't stay out of the investigation because of that," she stated in a determined voice.

He laughed. "Let me know how far that gets you."

She turned, gave him a flat stare, and added, "Oh, don't worry about me. I'll get where I need to go."

"Watch it," he warned in a gentle voice. "You're starting to sound like Eric."

She winced at that. "Right, that determination at all costs?"

"Something like that," he confirmed, with a nod, "yet ten times worse, and, because he could do everything, you never doubted whatever he said he would do."

She nodded. "And yet I don't remember him ever being totally obnoxious."

"Not totally obnoxious, no"—Nikolai laughed—"but plenty obnoxious."

"That's a problem too. It's never easy when you have all these personalities, living in stressful situations, and people start going behind your back, grouping with like minds, and if you happen to be on the wrong side of all of that," she murmured, "it doesn't look good for you."

"Sure, but no way you can't be on the wrong side of somebody." Nikolai shrugged. "When you look around, and you see how much chaos is happening, there will be sides. You have to keep sticking to the side of right, and hopefully the rest of it will work out."

"I wonder," she murmured, looking over at him. "When you say the *side of right*, what does that even mean?"

"Everybody here thinks they're in the right," he admitted pointedly, "except for whoever helped Eric pull off this shit. And, if he didn't help Eric pull off this crap, he must have some suspicion of what Eric had been up to."

"You do realize that, when it comes to that kind of thinking, everybody here will think that *you're* the one who knew something and who still has something to hide."

DAY 2 MORNING

EMILY LOOKED FROM Bertie, the big Samoyed cross that she was brushing, to Joe, walking toward her with a cup of coffee. He placed it beside her. "I know you're hiding," he stated, with a knowing stare, "so you might as well be warm and comfortable while you're doing so."

She gave a choked laugh, as she gently scratched Bertie's neck. "I wouldn't have said I was *hiding*," she muttered, "but everybody's going around and around again with the same damn information, and it's not getting us anywhere."

"Yeah, things can get like that." He checked the dog barn area and asked her casually, "You want to take them out for a ski?"

"Yes, absolutely I do." Emily bounded to her feet, laughing, as Bertie jumped around, barking.

"I'm taking Benji over there for some more exercise," Joe shared. "He's one of my two dogs that got shot. I'm not real happy with the way that leg is healing, and I suspect his sledding days are over."

"Oh, ouch, sorry about that."

"He's also seven, so maybe his days need to be over," Joe muttered, with a shrug. "Anyway, I need to take a bunch of them out. No games today."

"Do you take them out every day?"

"Of course," he confirmed, looking at her.

She nodded. "Anybody else come with you?"

"Lots of times, Magnus, Egan, Barret. Hell, everybody comes out and spends time with the dogs." Joe smiled and she laughed.

"I think that's selfishness on their part." She bent over and gave Bertie a big hug. "I love having the dogs here."

He grinned. "I know. I have the best seat in the house. Unfortunately too many shenanigans are happening at the base to make me happy. So, I'm okay to stay here and to keep hidden away." Joe shrugged. "Whatever the hell's going on with that base is bad news."

"I know," she agreed. "I don't want to be scared all the time, but it's hard not to, especially when I'm there."

"Of course it is, with all the shit going on all the time." Joe added, "Doesn't mean that it's yours to deal with though. If you stay out of the shit, you might stay out of the line of fire."

"And yet I feel as if Nikolai's in the line of fire now, and that's not fair either."

"Did you put him there?" Joe asked her.

Surprised, she shook her head, as she helped Joe buckle the dogs on leads and then put on her own skis. She checked her bindings to make sure everything was good. "All good here. I think Whalen's been doing a lot of equipment checks."

Joe nodded. "He does appear to be quite bothered that something will go wrong with the equipment."

"I think he's being cautious," she noted, "and I, for one, appreciate it." She shook out her foot, clicked her ski on, and looked at Joe. "Are we taking Bertie? She's not on a leash."

"I'll take these three on a leash, and, of course, Benji has to come." He laughed. "The others can stay inside. Bertie too."

"They won't like that, will they?"

"I'll take them out a little bit later," Joe explained, "but we don't want to take them all out if we're skiing. We'll take four, and that's plenty."

"And if they get tired?"

"We're the only ones who will get tired—besides Benji, after getting shot, and he's one of the reasons I'm taking them out now."

"Got it," she said.

"Anyway, let's get a move on now, so we'll be back for dinnertime." With that, he opened the door and let out the dogs, then he turned to look back at the others and gave them a warning. "Stay inside. I'll be back in a little bit."

They didn't like that and started to howl the minute the door closed on them.

She looked around and frowned. "I hate to even leave them alone and locked up."

He stopped, frowned, and asked, "What do you mean?"

She shrugged. "I don't know, just one of those ghostly feelings over my back," she muttered. "As if… no, no, no, I won't even say it."

"Now you already put fear in my head." He pulled out his phone and faced her. "I need somebody to come sit with the dogs. Who do you suggest?"

"Nikolai. He needs a break."

"And is he trustworthy?"

"Absolutely." He studied her, and she shrugged. "No, I don't have a reason to say that, but neither do I have any reason to think he's not safe. I've been watching him from a distance for quite a while," she shared. "I think he's as real as it gets."

"I'll take your word for it."

As soon as Nikolai answered the phone, Joe explained he was heading out for some skiing with the dogs and with Emily and wanted Nikolai to stay with the remaining dogs to ensure that everything was safe. Joe looked over at Emily, as he put away his phone. "He did sound relieved."

"Exactly. Everybody's looking at him sideways now. He was friends with Eric, good friends supposedly, but now Nikolai's wondering if they were friends at all."

Joe winced. "Got to love those scenarios, don't we?"

"Not really." She gave a shake of her head. "It's tough enough that he's already wondering what happened to his friend, but now he's also got to be wondering if he himself was set up or if his friend was deliberately using Nikolai. Now that? ... *That* kind of betrayal is hard."

"Yeah, the thing about trust is, the minute you lose it, it feels like a betrayal. So, in Nikolai's case, I'm sure he does feel very much as if he's been used."

As they moved across the snow, Emily studied the vast whiteness around them, her skis crisply sliding across the surface. "I guess we have more snow coming in tonight, don't we? Seems more storms are coming in the next couple days."

Joe nodded. "Yeah, that's one of the reasons I wanted to get these dogs out for a bit. They're all quite happy to be couch potatoes, but they also love to get out for a run." Sure enough, the dogs were running quite nicely beside them and in front of them.

"What about their pads on the snow?" she asked.

"That's another thing I'm checking," Joe said. "They've all got on different pad protectors today, ones that I've been developing for out here, so that their claws can go through but it still protects their soles and their pads from the ice. Some breeds do really well naturally on ice. Some breeds don't, and you get weaknesses within the purebreds as well. Every once in a while, you get one where his pad gets cut up," Joe noted. "Of course then you're leaving a blood trail, which isn't smart."

She winced at that. As they forged ahead, she looked around and smiled. "This really is one of those vast places where Mother Nature totally rules, isn't it?"

"Yes," Joe agreed. "It's one of the last frontiers in many ways."

"I was thinking of the ocean in that way," she shared, sending him a chuckle. "So much land that we have explored and so much ocean that we haven't. It always amazes me that we can have so much dedication to one aspect and not the rest."

"Oh, I agree with you there," Joe replied. "Although my dogs love to swim, the ocean isn't exactly where my heart is."

"What about retirement? Any thoughts of that in the near future?"

"Oh, I think about it," he admitted, with a huff. "Certainly on this trip I've thought about it a lot."

She looked over at the older man and realized that the years were creeping on him. "You're probably past the normal age of retirement anyway." He glared at her, and she laughed. "I'm not trying to insult you, but I suspect you've been pushing the line for a while."

"My wife would agree with that," he muttered, with half a smile, "absolutely she would."

As Emily looked around, and they talked generally about his family life and the fact that his wife wanted him to retire and to stay home, Emily pointed out something dark in the distance. "Do we know what that is?"

"No, not yet, and the guys were out looking for tracks this morning, but I'm not sure anybody saw anything. The guys' tracks didn't go this direction, although they probably did a circle around."

"And yet," she added, "it's pretty hard to see anything, especially when everything seems to give you a white outlook."

"It can be hard to see out here," he admitted, "particularly if you're at the wrong angle. Even something buried first appears as a hump in the snow but still could easily become invisible again, depending on what you use as a landmark or an anchor to hold down sightings," he explained.

Emily added, "I wouldn't be at all surprised if people aren't out looking for any sign of Teegan, with some renewed hope, now that Eric survived out here for so long. I think Mountain led a group out earlier."

Joe laughed. "Mountain has already combed this area many, many times, looking for any sign of his brother. So, if he's got any hope that Eric's survival is connected to his brother Teegan's, then Mountain will be out here."

"I wouldn't be surprised," she muttered. Even as they skied miles away from the base, she couldn't help but keep looking behind her to ensure that her tracks were there.

"If you're nervous, we can head back," Joe suggested calmly.

"No, it's fine," she muttered, feeling a deep sense of unease. "I just got that feeling of wrongness again."

"Ah, the one that had me phoning your friend to keep an eye on the dogs?"

"That one, yeah. We're out here, in the vastness of this

world …"

They skied a little bit farther, and she pointed, "I keep thinking I'm seeing something over there."

"Let's go then." Joe immediately turned his skies in that direction.

"You didn't see anything though," she noted. "I hate to make this a wild goose chase."

He snorted. "I'm out here exercising dogs. I don't care if we go left, right, straight, or do circles around this cursed place. If you pick a particular direction you want to go, let's go. I don't mind, and these dogs certainly don't. Exercise is exercise, no matter what."

With that, they veered ever-so-slightly off to the side. As they got closer and closer, he pointed to the circle and said, "I see it too."

At that confirmation, they spurred their skis to go faster and faster, until they came upon an odd sight. She kicked off her skis and walked over, until she was crouched in front of what appeared to be a temporary campsite. She looked over at Joe. "I don't like the look of this," she muttered.

"Maybe it's not a case of we don't appreciate the look of it, but maybe this is where Eric had been hiding out."

She nodded and pulled out her phone. Then they heard a shout from behind, and she turned, Mountain coming toward them.

When he reached them, his gaze immediately took in the surroundings, and he whistled. "I saw you guys veer off back there, and obviously you'd found something," he muttered.

"I don't know what we found." Emily shrugged and then pointed to the makeshift campsite. "I was about to call you."

Mountain nodded. "And it's a good thing that, whatever

this is, we got here to see it up close. Let me take a quick look." He kicked off his skis and walked over very quickly, investigating the site.

Emily noted that the shelter had been dug down quite a way into the snowpack and was quite hollow but covered with white plastic tarping and built as if an igloo. Plus she saw the remnant of a fire, and even sleeping bags and food were inside the snow cave. She asked Mountain, "Do you think this is where Eric was living?"

He stared at it for a long moment and then looked back at her intently. "Somebody certainly was. I hope it was him."

"As versus anybody else?" she asked. "Because you don't want to think anybody else is involved with Eric?"

"God, no. Obviously I really want to find my brother, but I can't imagine that he would have been stuck here for any particular reason."

"How do you track … Is there any chance that more than one person was here, though?" Joe asked from behind them.

She looked around, shaking her head. "I don't know how you can," she muttered, as she stared at the surrounding area. "It's also almost sheer ice here," she said, pointing to the shininess.

"That's because he's used water or heat," Mountain replied, studying the area, "in order to make it glassy, probably specifically to hide his tracks."

She stared at him and then nodded. "That makes a sick kind of sense. I hadn't considered that."

"For that reason alone, I'm pretty sure this would have been Eric's campsite," Mountain stated. "And it's huge to find out where he's been staying." As he looked around again, he nodded. "It's also very well-thought-out. It would appear to be a blind fissure that no one would typically notice, even passing right by it, not to mention from farther away." He pulled out his phone. "I'll bring out Magnus and maybe Barret or some of the others to take a closer look." He looked at Emily and stated, a bit too sternly, "Don't tell anybody about this."

She winced. "What about Nikolai?"

"Not yet," Mountain stated firmly. "I'll tell him myself." She hesitated, and he looked at her, understanding her hesitation. "I will."

"Fine," she replied, "but he does need to know and soon. He's tearing himself apart over this."

He looked at her carefully and asked, "And that matters to you?"

Surprised, she shrugged. "It should matter to all of us. Everybody's had a hard time over this, some more than others. In his case, I think, with Eric's betrayal, Nikolai's reassessing if he even knew this guy."

"I think we're all doing that to some degree," Mountain admitted. "So, yeah, my sympathies are with Nikolai, and I certainly understand what betrayal is like."

She nodded. "In many ways, I think we've all had an experience with betrayal that didn't make any of us like humanity any better, but I do know that Nikolai's particularly affected, and yet he's hiding it. I don't think he would appreciate it if he knew that everyone could see how he's feeling."

"No, I'm sure not," Mountain agreed. "We're all feeling the tension, aren't we?"

"We are," she confirmed.

He studied her closely again. In a low voice, making sure Joe was out of hearing, Mountain asked her, "Mason sent you, didn't he?" When she stared at him for a long moment, he nodded, almost to himself. "You don't have to say anything. The look in your eye was enough."

"If it was enough," she said, "then I've already failed."

"Nope, not at all, but I am interested at the change of tactic."

"I think he was afraid you guys were causing too much interest. And I can be more easily overlooked."

"Maybe. ... Not to worry. I won't say anything. But realize that—you working secretly for Mason—might be ultimately seen by Nikolai as if it's a betrayal too."

She shrugged. "I don't know him that well, certainly not enough for something to come between us," she shared. "And, if it does, it's really not an issue."

He chuckled. "If only I had a dollar for every time somebody said something similar to me… but believe me. Nikolai will want to be on the inside track, as soon as you feel clear enough to tell him."

"I can't do that," she said, "and you know that."

"I do know that," he replied, with a smirk. "So the road that you're heading down right now won't be easy."

"Sure," she conceded, "but, if it helps bring an end to all this death and mayhem, it'll be worth it." And, with that, she headed off to where Joe had been dealing with the dogs.

As Joe looked up, she said, "Seems it's time for us to go home. Mountain's called a couple men out here."

"Good," Joe replied. "This isn't where we belong anyway."

She smiled and nodded. "I won't argue with that. We found something important though, and now we can head back." She quickly clicked on her skis, waited until Joe had the dogs ready, and they headed back toward the base again.

The trip seemed much faster because Joe had taken the lead and had chosen a far more direct route than the more meandering path they had taken earlier.

When they reached the dog barn, Emily helped Joe get the dogs settled in. After they had put the dogs inside, she announced, "I'll go grab a hot cup of tea before dinner."

He nodded and then asked, "You want to go back out again tomorrow?"

She beamed. "I'm all for it."

He grinned at her. "It's nice to have somebody come along who can keep up but not make me look as if I'm old and infirm."

At that, she burst out laughing. "Yeah, that's not happening. You're incredibly fit, though I know that a few of these guys make all of us look like idiots. Yet I consider myself in pretty good shape," she admitted. "Still, something about being with a group of the military's elite men makes me want to curl up and cry because I'm not at that level of strength."

Joe shook his head. "You're doing damn well, so don't let anybody make you feel any differently. Don't be so hard on yourself."

She smiled her thanks, and, after a big cuddle with Bertie, Emily quickly made her escape. Instead of getting tea, she headed straight for her room. Once there, she shut the door and quickly phoned Mason. It took a bit for the call to go through, but, as soon as he answered, she admitted, "I've already been made. I told you that I wasn't any good at this."

After a short silence on the other end, he asked, "Made by whom?"

"Mountain."

He chuckled, seemingly enjoying the revelation. "Yeah, I

would expect nothing less of him, and, besides, I warned him that I was tapping somebody he wouldn't expect, so he's been looking at who was there to see what else I could come up with for assistance."

"Yeah, well, I'm hardly anybody who you can really tap," she argued. "The investigative work I've always done has been secretive, such as this."

"And that's the beauty of it. You're undercover, and nobody suspects you because you're already there," Mason stated in a warm tone. "Don't you worry about Mountain. He won't say anything to anybody. Besides, it's enough for him that you're on his side."

"Sure, but I can't really let anybody know I'm on his side."

"Nope, and that's always the trick," Mason confirmed, with a smile in his voice. "Now you just keep being who you are, who you've been all along, but keep your eyes and ears open, and let me know what's going on."

She hesitated.

Mason understood her reluctance. "Relax, Emily. Of all the people who need to know, Mountain's probably the perfect one, so just do you and believe it will be fine." And, with that, he hung up.

Groaning, she left her room and headed toward the kitchen to get that tea. She needed it even more now. The chill from outside, combined with working up quite a sweat, had now settled a little deeper into her soul, as she thought about what she was doing and what Mason had requested from her. She had talked to him many times over the years but hadn't seen him in person in years.

That she had nobody to talk to was a problem, nobody at all, though maybe Mountain now, yet that was dangerous too. Voices could be heard in this place, as she well knew. A little too easily, she thought, not that she'd heard anything particularly useful yet, though she'd been careful so far, and sure didn't want to get caught trying to listen in on conversations. People here were already stressed to the max and not quick to trust, and plenty of them seemed as if they wouldn't be very forgiving.

NIKOLAI SAT AT a dining room table in the corner, talking with some random guys about all the base shenanigans. A couple of them were pumping him as to what the hell had gone wrong with Eric, but Nikolai didn't have an answer. He'd given it no small amount of thought, but he just didn't know, and he'd been pretty blunt about it. He thought most of them would take him at his word, but he didn't know what they would say to each other, once they walked out of here.

As it was, several of them got up and were heading back to their rooms for a few minutes before dinner. Nikolai nodded, and, with some genial conversation coming to an end, he sat in place and waited until they were gone. Almost immediately Emily walked in, scanned the room, and, taking one look at him, smiled and walked over.

"Hey. How you doing?" she asked.

He shrugged. "I'm sure you know how I'm doing."

"If I had to guess, I would say that you're doing okay, but you've been better."

He laughed. "Exactly." He looked at her, curious. "How was skiing with Joe and the dogs?"

"Good, great to be out. Thanks for checking in on the

other dogs while we were gone. Hope I didn't overstep, but, when he asked if I could suggest someone, I thought you might enjoy the break."

"I did, thanks. Find anything?" he asked, going straight to the point, his gaze sharp.

She shrugged. "Maybe, not too sure. I didn't really go out there looking for anything." She gave a half laugh. "Joe was going and asked if I wanted to tag along. Jeez, that guy is in great shape. I am chilled though and need to go grab a hot drink."

"Go get something," he urged, "then get back here and talk to me."

She winced. "I can't say anything, though I was told that somebody will be talking to you about it."

His mouth snapped shut, and he looked at her quizzically.

She shrugged. "I can't even tell you if it's good news or bad. Let me get some tea at least." She headed over to the counter and quickly made her tea.

Chrissy looked over at her and smiled. "Dinner will be ready soon."

"Good," Emily said. "I could do with a hot soup."

"You've been outside today? It's pretty cold out there."

"Yeah, you're not kidding." Emily groaned. "I've been out skiing with Joe and the dogs."

"Oh, that's lovely. I miss that."

"Skiing with Joe?" Emily asked.

"Yes, believe it or not, I used to go out with the dogs a fair bit. I still sneak over and cuddle with the dogs. One there I really love, *Patches*, so I try to see her as often as I can."

"That makes sense to me," Emily murmured. "It's a

lovely way to spend the afternoon, and it wasn't as cold as it could have been. The trouble is, now that I'm inside, I'm having trouble getting warm again."

"Yeah, that's how it works," Chrissy noted cheerfully. "Get yourself a hot drink, sit down, and give your body a chance to recover."

And that's what Emily did, heading back to where Nikolai sat. As she looked at him, she smiled and casually said, "Don't look so worried."

"How else would I look, after what you just told me? Surely you didn't think it would make me feel better."

She nodded, then leaned forward and in a very low voice told him, "Not a word to anyone else. Since Mountain will be talking to you, you damn-well better be surprised when he tells you." She took a deep breath. "We think we may have found where Eric was camped."

Nikolai's eyebrows shot up, and air of excitement whispered across his face. "Oh, I'm glad to hear that."

"As I said, you don't know anything, and Mountain will talk to you."

"Got it." Nikolai stared around the room and shook his head. "I've been talking to the guys a lot today, yet always with that sense of looking at me for an explanation. However, I don't have anything to give them."

"And then you're stressing yourself out because you don't have an explanation, and it's killing you because, of all the people here, you should be the one who would have known. Or so you thought."

"Yes, exactly." He looked at her and around them several times. "It almost makes me think you're in the investigative business—or at least know humanity better than most."

She snorted. "I definitely know humanity, starting with

multiple brothers." She gave Nikolai a smile. "You can bet life with them has never been easy, but it's always been something to remember."

He smiled. "I kind of felt that way about Eric too. I would have said we were like brothers."

"And yet I'm sure you've felt something different this last little while."

"Yeah, he was more arrogant than usual," Nikolai muttered, "held more disgust for humans in general, including those around him. I finally told him to ease up. That was the only argument we ever had," he admitted. "Then he told me to stop being such a prick and to own up to the fact that everybody here was half of what we were, and, if I wasn't so righteous, he would be talking to me more too. I never understood what he meant by that, and now I'm sitting here wondering if I didn't miss a clue."

"Sounds as if maybe you did," she noted in a sympathetic tone, "but then you weren't looking for a clue. Why would you?"

"No, and still I should have been," he admitted. "Honestly I need to talk to somebody, but I'm not sure how to get a hold of him. I'm not even sure if he's the right person."

"I don't know who you're looking for, but Mountain might know. Hell, I might even know," she suggested.

"He's somebody I worked with in Europe," Nikolai began. "He was pretty big in the military over here. I doubt he's got anything to do with this, but …"

"What's his name?" she asked, with a sinking feeling.

He looked at her, shrugged, and said, "Mason."

"Ah, why don't you talk to Mountain about it? He could probably make it happen. And, if you think there's a purpose for it, maybe he would do it."

"I don't know, but I feel as if I'm in a spot of trouble, and, if anybody could help me right now, it would be him. I met him on a couple overseas deployments."

"Then call him," she urged.

"I don't know how to get a hold of him," Nikolai said.

"Talk to Mountain. I think he's pretty good friends with him. Although I could be wrong." She frowned. "Maybe that was Magnus. Although, if Mountain feels a justification for it, I suspect he could put you in touch with just about anyone."

"Maybe… we'll see." Nikolai gave her half a smile. "I might have some way to do it on my own." And, with that, he stood and said, "Get warm." Then he quickly disappeared.

DAY 2 LATE MORNING

SWEARING TO HERSELF, she quickly contacted Mason via text. **He's looking for you. Nikolai. He knows you, thinks you might be the one to help him out.**

Help him out how?

Yeah, that would be between you two.

He called her and, in a low voice, asked if she was clear to talk.

"I'm in the dining area, and I'm all alone."

"That area always has eyes and ears, so don't ever believe that."

"No, I get that. I was explaining where I am."

"When did he say this?"

"A few minutes ago."

"What's his last name?"

"No idea," she replied cheerfully, "but he knew you. Told me how he'd done several training missions with you in Europe."

"Nikolai, *huh*? ... Oh, six-two or so, blond, blue eyes? Scar on the right side of his chin?"

"Yeah, that's him."

"Damn, I didn't know it was *that* Nikolai. If it's him, then I definitely know him. I'll call him." And, with that, he hung up.

She stared at the phone, shaking her head, wondering if

Nikolai would come back and talk to her or if this was a done deal for the night. When she looked up, Magnus strode toward her. He sat in front of her and said, "Something happened, and I don't know what."

"Lots of things happened, but I'm not sure what you're talking about," she replied.

"Why don't you fill me in?" She explained about the ski trip and what they'd found.

Magnus nodded, explaining that he'd sent the others out to the campsite, since he was tied up here. Then she'd explained about Nikolai wanting to talk to Mason, and, at that, Magnus's eyebrows shot up, and then he laughed. "That figures. It seems as if Mason's getting to be pretty-damn popular."

"I haven't seen the man myself in a couple years. The way our comms connection here sucks, it's not always that easy to get through, so I wouldn't be surprised if they *didn't* connect. I did tell Nikolai to talk to Mountain though."

Magnus smiled at that. "That's another good call," he agreed, and, to that, she didn't say anything.

She looked around and added, "I sure hope dinner is out soon." She tried to stifle a shiver. "I got a chill out there again." Immediately he frowned at her. She shrugged. "I'm fine. It's just that waiting for dinner now is putting me on edge."

"You could go ask for a bowl of something hot, if they have it."

"You also know that they don't appreciate it when you interrupt them with special requests, right when they're trying to get a meal out."

Almost immediately he smiled. Since her back was to the kitchen, she didn't know what was happening. Magnus laughed. "Somebody obviously noticed."

Sure enough, Emily turned to see Chrissy walking toward her, carrying a hot bowl of soup. Placing it in front of Emily, she smiled. "No, we don't do this all the time, so consider it a one-time deal. Don't tell anybody." Just like that, she was gone, leaving a very happy Emily behind.

⊕

IT DIDN'T TAKE long to connect, and that alone surprised Nikolai. When he finally did speak to Mason, he immediately greeted him with, "I'm in trouble."

Silence came on the other end for a moment, and then Mason replied, "Hello, Nikolai. It's been a long time."

"Yeah, it has been, and I am in trouble."

"I did hear about some of it," he began. "So, this guy who's been missing?"

"Eric. Yes."

"A friend of yours, right?"

"Yes," he replied cautiously, "but there are friends, and then there are friends, and apparently this is a friend I didn't really know. Not well enough anyway."

"Explain."

For the next few minutes, Nikolai gave Mason a firsthand accounting of what he thought his relationship with Eric had been. Then Nikolai added more at the end. "I should also say that I haven't had a whole lot to do with him in the last few years, and, when I saw him this time, it surprised me how much he'd changed."

"In what way?"

"More arrogant, more dismissive of the people around him, more dismissive of life. I don't know. He didn't look as if he played well with others anymore."

"That's probably because he didn't, I'm sure. Life gets to be a little too easy for some people, and I think they get careless and stop giving a crap about what other people think or do or say. As long as it doesn't interfere with their world, they allow it to be, but the minute it does impact their world, they can't handle it."

"That's a good description of where Eric was at."

"I have heard from a few people on the base," he shared, "and, just so you know, the investigation is ongoing. However, I don't have too much in the way of information yet."

"No, as of my last briefing—unofficially, of course—I heard that they may have found Eric's hiding place, a makeshift campsite, his hideout, but it's most likely where he had been staying."

"I did hear that today too," Mason confirmed, "but I have yet to talk to Mountain himself."

"Right, well, anyway I want to tell you that, if you have any influence in this godforsaken place... I didn't do anything wrong, and I'm bound and determined to help sort out what the hell Eric was up to and how much damage he's caused to the people here. Something is ... not *broken* but *revved up* may be a better word for it, as if Eric was finally doing something that he thought was worth his while. Yet, when he got here, he was the same incredibly arrogant, dismissive person I hadn't seen in a very long time."

"When did you see that before?"

"When we were in training. He could do everything, and I mean *everything*. He was so much better than anybody else. People both loved and hated him," Nikolai shared. "And that made for a very difficult lifestyle for him sometimes because a lot of people didn't have any patience for his brand of mockery and disgust." Nikolai sighed. "Anyway I wanted to let you know that I'm innocent, that I'm cooperating, and that I'm doing my own investigation here as well."

"Don't do anything stupid," Mason warned. "An awful lot of investigating is going on right now. I don't know that they're very close to finding any answers because of the nature of the problem, but I'm sure you probably know by now that Mountain is also looking for his brother."

"That would be one Teegan Rode," he stated.

"Exactly."

"Yeah, I knew that."

"Did you ever see any interactions between Teegan and Eric?"

"Interactions?"

"Yes, as in talking, laughter, mockery, anything that would spell trouble?"

Nikolai sat back and thought about it. "I don't know that it necessarily spelled trouble, but Eric was very much of the opinion that Teegan was a green kid, still wet behind the ears."

"He was, in a way, but that wasn't his fault. He was young and hadn't had a chance to learn and experience that much yet, is all."

"I know. I know, but, for Eric, it wouldn't have mattered. That still would have been something Eric would have been pretty mocking about."

"Doesn't seem to be a very nice guy."

"Eric didn't used to be such an asshole, honestly. ... He was good to work with, before all this mess. So the fact that he had become such an asshole in this situation is kind of disturbing because that wasn't him before."

"Maybe not, but sounds as if it's him now."

"And yet, I swear to you, that's not the man I knew before."

"Okay, yet you can't think of any conversation or anything between Teegan and Eric?"

"Oh, wait, hang on a minute," he murmured. "Some sort of betting was going on."

At that, Mason let out a hard breath. "You mean, about staying outside long enough without getting killed and that type of thing, more the workings of daredevils?"

"Yeah, a bunch of that kind of talk was going on. I'm not sure if Eric was part of that, but I definitely remember Teegan laughing about a bunch of it."

"Yeah, he would, but I would hope he wouldn't rise to the bait."

"Around here though, what that's like?" Nikolai asked, with a cautious tone. "If you don't rise to the bait, they'll try harder and harder to get you to give in."

Silence came on the other end, and Mason finally responded, "Look. You do your investigation but keep Mountain in the loop. That's the only way to keep your ass clear of trouble."

"Is he the one running this? What about Samson and Ted?"

"Yes, they are running the more overt investigation. Don't forget a CO's on top."

"We never see him much, especially lately. I'm not sure he comes out of his room at all anymore. The colonel is more of a mystery than this place."

"I'm pretty sure he thinks this assignment is a punishment, and he's just putting in his time, until he's done," Mason noted. "All I can tell you is, you have to keep your nose clean right now, particularly while everybody is under so much stress about your supposed good friend because everybody'll be looking to you for answers."

"They already are," Nikolai admitted. "I don't have any to give, but it doesn't stop them all from looking at me as if I can give them the winning lottery ticket numbers or something," he replied bitterly.

"And speaking of which," Mason asked, "did your friend leave anything behind at the base? Was anything left for you, a note, a message? A favorite something or other? Anything?"

"No, and that was one of the reasons why I knew that something must have happened to him because he didn't say anything, coming or going. He was here one moment, and then he was gone."

"So that wouldn't have been normal behavior?"

"It wasn't normal behavior from a few years ago, but remember. I hadn't seen him since then. I had talked to him occasionally. We chatted every once in a while, but definitely a distance grew between us. And he did say something about, if I wasn't so righteous, he could have brought me in on some deals over time. But, when I laughed and reminded him that his kind of deals weren't my kind of deals … Eric gave me that same mocking attitude, as if to say, *Poor me*, and then he was gone again."

"That's the problem of course. We're all wondering what kind of deals he was involved in on this assignment and how much those deals impacted his disappearance. Yet he didn't disappear. Apparently he stepped out and stayed out."

"And see? That's the part I don't get."

"Believe me. That's what none of us get. What was the reason? What was the advantage? How did hanging around the base, yet not being a part of the base, benefit him?"

As the two of them thought about it, finally Nikolai reluctantly added, "It allowed him the anonymity to do anything he wanted. By distancing himself from the others, he just did his thing."

Mason sucked in his breath, followed by a sigh of sorrow, as if his worse thoughts were voiced. "That's what I was thinking. Now comes the tough question, and I need you to be as clear and as honest as you can be. Would Eric turn around and kill somebody, regardless of the team, regardless of what was happening? Would he do it for money? Would he do it for the thrill? Would he do it just because—"

Absolutely no hesitation came in Nikolai's mind, as he immediately interrupted, "He would… yes, absolutely, and I'm pretty sure he's already done it."

"Any proof of that?" Mason asked.

"No, I don't have any proof," Nikolai stated, "none at all, but we were at a separate training session—this one was in Alaska," he added. "Two men died during the training."

"Which happens," Mason conceded. "I wish to God it didn't, but we all know that, every once in a while, things go wrong."

"Yeah, things went wrong all right, but, in both cases, Eric was there. He told me how the trainees were idiots, and how all he had to do was prove it to them, and how that had been as easy as pie. When I asked him if he'd done anything to kill those men, he looked at me in his most mocking way. He told me that he didn't have to, that they were idiots. All he had to do was give them the opportunity to hang themselves, and they would have done it."

At that, silence came on the other end, and Mason finally spoke. "Okay, give me details on that trip. We'll need to look hard at this friend of yours and confirm any information that can be found in his history. We must find it and find it fast."

"Why?" Nikolai asked. "Eric's dead and gone. He can't give us any more answers."

"Oh, he'll have answers, if only to help understand the mind-set of a killer who doesn't give a crap," Mason noted, with a sharp tone. "Remember. Lots of people have died at that base this session, and we need to know how much, if anything, your friend had to do with it."

"To start with, stop calling Eric *my friend*," Nikolai said, "and I'll start digging into the past and get you as much information as I have. I don't even think a lot of it's on record because he was there, but often on secret missions for his own team. I'm not even sure that Eric would consider what he did as being wrong. I think he would consider it fair game, and God help us if he did have anything to do with the deaths here. That is not something I want on my shoulders."

"It isn't on your shoulders," Mason declared. "That's never been on your shoulders. It's on Eric's."

Mason may have said it, but Nikolai knew in his heart that he was as much part of it as Eric was.

DAY 2 DINNER

EMILY LOOKED FROM her soup, as Nikolai raced back in the dining room. He saw her, stopped for a moment, then determinedly walked toward her. He sat with a *thud* across from her and leaned closer. "I spoke to Mason."

"Oh, good," she replied. "I'm glad you got through so quickly."

He nodded. "As I mentioned, we're acquaintances. I didn't realize that he might have anything to do with this place."

She gave him a wry look. "Not a whole lot Mason *doesn't* have a hand in," she noted. "Whether he likes it or not, he gets tapped for a lot of troubleshooting."

Nikolai nodded at that. "He's asked me to dredge up information from Eric's past that I know about, but I never really said anything about," he admitted. "I did report something to my CEO at the time, but it was completely dismissed as being ludicrous. But now I need to get some paper, pen, or maybe even a laptop would be better." He looked at her intently. "Do you have anything?"

Frowning, she nodded. "Yeah, I have a laptop."

"Good, that's a good place to start.

"Do you want a hand with jogging your memories, writing it all down?"

He hesitated and then nodded. "If you're up for it, but it

could be ugly."

"Hey, everything I've seen so far has been ugly," she stated. "If this gives us a head start on anything, I'm all for it. Besides, your friend is gone."

He winced. "I know it's a long shot, but any chance I could get you to not call Eric *my friend* anymore?" She was not surprised at his request. "I'm starting to realize I didn't know this man at all."

"Absolutely," she said. "Do you want dinner first?"

He nodded, then looked around. "How about we go to your room afterward, then nobody will think anything of it—outside of thinking we have a relationship going on?"

"That's fine," she agreed smoothly. "Let's eat first, and then I'll take more hot tea back to my room."

"You're really cold, aren't you?" he asked, concern in his voice.

"Yeah, but I'm not sure how much is actual cold versus the feeling of wondering who this Eric person was."

"Yeah, I'm starting to realize that he was a whole lot less than I thought and a whole lot more than I wanted."

Surprised, she watched as Nikolai rose, walked over to grab some food, and then returned and sat down beside her. "You'll need more than that soup."

"I was planning on getting more," she shared, "but the lineup is starting."

He shrugged. "Here. Help yourself to this, and I'll go get more." And, with that, he dashed off again. She was surprised when he came back with a full plate, way more than he could eat.

"So, you expect me to eat all this?" she asked, looking at the amount of food on her plate.

He stared at it and shrugged. "Honestly I got what I

would have eaten and then some."

"I'm glad to hear that because you'll be eating leftovers at this rate."

He grinned, and, looking suddenly boyish, he laughed. "I don't think leftovers are a problem."

"I hope not"—she smirked—"because no way I can eat all this." She was quite surprised when, twenty minutes later, her plate was way more than half empty.

He teased her, "What's this about not being able to eat? Looks to me as if you're doing a pretty good job on it."

"I can't believe I ate that much," she admitted, rubbing her tummy. "I hope I'm not sick all night."

He shook his head. "No reason to be sick. Besides, the food's good."

"I know. Chef's great, isn't he?"

"He is."

At that, Elijah, the chef, who had walked out to check everything, heard the comment. He walked over and noted, "Okay, so you guys obviously heard about dessert, and you're angling for a piece already."

She looked at him and batted her eyes. "A piece of pie, a piece of something sweet, would be lovely," she replied, with a laugh. "We're heading back to my room after this, so I can get under the covers and get warm."

Chef frowned. "Chrissy told me that you were chilled." He eyed her carefully. "It's not smart dilly-dallying in this weather."

"Yeah, thanks," she muttered, with an eye roll. "I'm pretty sure I didn't do it on purpose."

"You don't have to around here," he stated, with a nod. "It's pretty easy to catch a chill, whether you thought you would get one or not." He came back a few minutes later with a plate of two still-warm slices of chocolate cake with chocolate pudding flowing from the center. She stared at it and wondered, "Is that a lava cake?"

He laughed. "Yeah, it is. You can thank Chrissy for these." And, with that, he was gone.

She stared at the treat in delight, looked over at Nikolai, and grinned. "I don't know about you, but it's pretty hard to let go of this."

Nikolai smiled. "I guess that's the advantage of having somebody like Chrissy here. I've never really had quite such baking on a base before this. The cookies and stuff were good before, but she's definitely raised the baking game."

"I know. She does pretty amazing stuff." Emily looked at him and grinned. "Besides, it gives us a chance to bond over sweets."

He rolled his eyes. "Do we need to bond?"

"*Need*, no," she replied, batting her eyes, "but we've already started—in case you hadn't noticed."

He laughed hard at that. "You are by far one of the friendliest in this group."

"I think fear has divided everybody," she murmured, "and that's a tough thing to change too. As we solve some of these issues, I'm hoping it'll help smooth out everything."

"What are you doing after this?" he asked.

"Going wherever I'm sent," she stated, with a smile.

"You're staying in the military long-term?"

"Yeah." She considered that for a moment and then clarified, "Although I'm wondering about doing some schooling and training and getting out at some point in time. Eventually I want a family and all that, but right now? This is where I want to be. It's a career path for me, and we'll see afterward." He nodded. "What about you?" she asked him curiously. "Are you going back to Switzerland?"

"No, I don't think so," he shared, as he shifted around and looked at the rest of the place, buzzing with muttering voices and hushed whispers. "I need to make peace with all this, and I'm not sure what form that'll take."

"Can't make peace until we solve it," she noted. "Closure is probably a requirement."

"And yet a lot of people don't ever get closure to traumatic events in their lives," he pointed out.

"I know," she agreed, "and I can imagine that it must be like an itch that never goes away. I don't want that to be you either," she added, after a moment.

He looked over at her. "We've hardly even talked the whole time we've been here."

"We have though," she corrected, with a laugh, "while playing lots of cards and some board games."

"But you always kept your distance."

"You kept your distance," she pointed out. When he frowned at her, she nodded. "The minute Eric disappeared, you retreated into yourself. So, what I had thought was a potential friendship opening up was then changed, and you kind of disappeared in a way too. I wasn't exactly sure if you would ever come back," she admitted. "Kind of hard to watch actually."

He kept staring at her, as if shocked, and she was surprised that she had shared this, but she meant it. Everything she'd known of him up until now she'd really liked, but it had been almost impossible to get to know Nikolai because he'd been hidden behind this wall of protection, as if afraid or maybe even looking at trying to minimize the hurt he felt.

She smiled. "That's all right. No pressure."

"No pressure?" he asked wearily.

"No pressure for a relationship," she clarified, with a chuckle, "because I thought you were downright cute and thought maybe we had something going, but you backed off. Still, that doesn't mean you have to pick up there again. I'm not against it, but I know that, for a lot of people, I'm a little too forward … and in your face. I don't want to say *aggressive* because I would hate to think that I *was* aggressive." She pondered the lava cake in front of her, wondering why she was even going down this road, except that it was who she was. She was honest to a fault, and, if she wanted something, she went after it.

But when he had backed off so quickly back then, it had been obvious that he was so hurt by Eric's disappearance. After he had shut the door in her face so firmly, she hadn't really known what to do back then. As she looked over at him today, she could see that he still didn't know what to do with her. She grinned and added, "Honestly don't worry about it."

He shook his head. "I'm not worried. I'm flabbergasted because I didn't see it."

"No… you didn't see it, and I didn't want you to see it. I thought that maybe you would pull back out of the slump you were in and that life would improve for you. Instead you've stayed isolated, and now, with this latest hit, you're struggling even more."

He stiffened and silently glared at her.

She grinned. "Okay, fine. You don't like that terminology, and maybe *struggling* isn't the word, but it does seem as if you're missing out on an awful lot of opportunities. Listen. Eric is not you, so you are not responsible for Eric's actions. Eric is responsible for this, not you."

"But everybody here will think that I had something to

do with it. Even now they're always looking at me," he muttered, as he glanced around.

He was right, and she didn't need to see people staring openly or ducking behind them to know this to be true.

"I don't have any way of showing them that I didn't."

"That's why you need to talk to Mountain, Magnus, and the people who can help you."

He looked at her with a narrowed gaze, and she gave him a sunny smile back. "I know. You don't know what to do with me, and that's fine. I'm kind of used to that."

He shook his head. "I don't know how you can be fine with it. How come you're so open and trusting?" And then he stopped and guessed, "That's because you haven't been hurt in this life."

"Oh, I have been hurt," she countered, "multiple times in different ways, but I've also decided that I wouldn't let those hurts define who I am. You would do well to remember that."

"Would I?"

"You would. Most people hide away when they get hurt, and I did for a while. Then I realized that, by doing so, I was giving away my power to somebody who no longer appreciated who I was, and I vowed that I wouldn't do it anymore," she declared. "And, if you don't want anything to do with me, that's fine, really. I'm not trying to push myself into your space."

He gave her a crooked grin. "Are you sure?"

She burst out laughing and brought a bright smile to his face.

He shook his head. "You're like a ray of sunshine around this place. I keep looking for the deceit, for the ..." Then he stopped and stared at the plate in front of her. "I can't believe you ate most of that."

"I did," she declared, with a laugh.

"So, what now?"

"Let's go to my room, and we'll see what we can get done." She looked at him, waggled her eyebrows, and he flushed. Laughter peeled from her, making him shake his head and sling his arm through hers.

"How come I'm just seeing this now?"

"Because now," she noted cheerfully, "you're finally seeing me."

"And yet, when we first found Eric, you weren't terribly friendly."

"I was trying hard to shock you out of the reverie you were caught up in, what with all that pain, trying to figure out where and what was happening. You needed your head on straight for all the questions coming your way, and it was your way of dealing with this."

He stared at her and then nodded slowly. "Very true."

"If Eric was alive all that time, we're all hoping that Teegan is too."

"And Teegan is really what this is all about, isn't it?" He had asked it lightly, but his voice was nothing if not suspicious.

She stopped in the hallway, studied him, and said, "Teegan and I are friends, and that's it. Always have been, but with nothing between us." She poked Nikolai in the chest.

"Yeah, right."

She cut him off before he could say any more. "Listen to yourself, would you? Suspicion oozing out of every pore. Not sure who hurt you or why," she noted, "but that's not what's here and shouldn't be between us."

"There isn't anything between us," he pointed out.

"Because you won't give it a damn chance." At the look on his face, she burst out laughing. "I shouldn't tease you quite so badly."

"No, you shouldn't," he agreed, as he wrapped an arm around her shoulders and tucked her up close. "Yet it is very refreshing. Most people just avoid me."

"Yeah, and I've seen that happen here a lot." She chuckled. "Honestly I did too. I stayed away from you, as it seemed to be what you wanted. I buckled in and did what everybody else was doing, but it doesn't seem to be doing any good, and it's really not who I am," she shared. "So, there you go. From now on, I'll be me."

"Right, this irreverent bubbling you?"

"What? You didn't see the *bubbling* part before?" she asked.

He nodded. "I did. I just didn't really understand it." He shrugged. "My world hasn't heard much laughter lately."

"And that's the problem," she noted, "and that's why everybody was avoiding you, and now I won't. Because you ... kind of went into this weird dark place, where suddenly everything around you was wrong and suspicious. I don't know. ... It got *dark*, for lack of a better word."

"*Dark* works," he admitted, "and you're right. It was getting dark. Eric was a good friend of mine at one time, and I felt so damn guilty. I spent hours out there looking for him, and the fact that I didn't find him and that he was so close means that he was right all along—in that he had skills that he wasn't prepared to teach or to help anybody else with. Proof that he held himself as somehow better than everyone."

"A holier than thou kind of person," she agreed. "As you've explained, that's his personality, but what you don't understand is why he did it to you."

"And yet he's done it to me before. However, I didn't think he would do it in this context or to this extent," Nikolai explained. "The only thing I can think of is that … he was working with somebody else, and they had a reason for doing this, but no good reason comes to mind."

"It's well past the time to consider that," she stated lightly, and then looked around casually to see Mountain walking toward them.

"I need to talk to Nikolai," he said, his gaze going from her to him.

Nikolai nodded. "You might as well talk in front of her," he suggested. "Emily probably won't let me go with you anyway."

She burst out laughing. "I'm happy to be there, but I know that Mountain needs to talk to you."

Mountain studied her, then Nikolai. "You can stay," he decided, as he stared from one to other, trying to understand the dynamic at work here, and then nodded. "Sure, you can stay. It's not as if you weren't part of this."

And, with that, he motioned them both into one of the two meeting rooms that were available. As soon as they got inside, he closed the door then turned to Nikolai.

"Now, we need to talk."

✤

NIKOLAI LOOKED FROM Mountain to Emily. Nikolai still felt unsteady, after all the personal revelations from Emily, but, as she sat down, looking very much like the perky girl he had seen a while back—yet somehow hadn't seen since—he realized that maybe she was right about them. He was looking through a cloud of betrayal, anguish, and anger, all while he wasn't at all sure what the hell was going on.

However, as he looked at Mountain, Nikolai saw clarity and some animosity in that gaze. "I don't know what Eric was doing or how he perpetrated this," Nikolai began.

Mountain gave a clipped nod and quickly told him about finding Eric's campsite. "We have now conducted a full investigation into the site where he was staying. He had himself quite a campsite. It also explains some of the theft that's been going on here, plus he's been hunting. So, he was keeping himself supplied just fine."

"And he would have. He would have been absolutely and totally fine, short of somebody having dropped in on him unexpectedly. Yet he was well hidden out there. ... I still don't understand why."

"So, to answer that, I need you to think hard about any conversations he had with you, any mentions, anything out of the ordinary at all, anything about working with somebody else, championing somebody else, or somebody else being involved in something, anything at all that would give you some idea of what he was doing out there and why."

"I *have* been considering all that," he declared in an exasperated tone. "As I mentioned before, Eric did say something about, if I wasn't quite so honorable, he would bring me in on a deal, but I assumed he meant something outside of this base."

"And yet ... what if it wasn't?"

"Sure, but who would be involved? Someone on this base or somebody around this base?" Nikolai asked, thinking of the scientists' camp or the local villagers, and then he stopped. "Why wouldn't he have just gone to the scientists' camp and holed up there?"

"Probably because we're still tracking it," Mountain noted in a grating tone. "We go over there every couple days. The movement would have been noticed."

"Right." Nikolai dropped his head. "So, Eric deemed his privacy was more important than his comfort."

"If it weren't, he never would have left," Emily pointed out in a quiet voice.

Nikolai frowned at her absentmindedly and then nodded. "I can't imagine what Eric was up to, but he was the kind of guy who would play a lot of war games, even mind games. But would this have been a game? I don't think so." Nikolai shook his head. "I can't imagine what game there could possibly be that he thought was worth doing this. If there were bets going on about who could stay out the longest? Maybe. But why would anybody choose to do that, knowing it would set off the entire base to search for any members deemed missing? If not killing several members doing the dare or involved in the searches."

At that, Mountain stared off in the distance, as if pondering that.

Emily asked Nikolai, "You don't really think that somebody would have done that, do you?" Yet her gaze went from Nikolai to Mountain.

"I don't know whether Eric would or not," Nikolai admitted, "but he would have had a lot of fun proving he could survive out there for long periods. I don't know. … Maybe if somebody he was particularly attached to had insulted him, maybe Eric would do this survival stunt as a way to walk back in triumphantly, as if to say, *Hey, look at what I did.*" Nikolai stood to pace the room. "But as to why Eric would attack Chrissy? I don't know." Nikolai shook his head. "Unless it wasn't her as much as Whalen."

"Why would anybody want to go up against Whalen?" Mountain asked, frowning at Nikolai.

"I don't know that anybody would," he replied. "I'm saying that, in a way, Eric had equal opportunity to kill either Chrissy or Whalen."

"So, Whalen… was he a threat to somebody? That's the question," Emily asked from her corner, where she sat looking from Mountain to Nikolai. "Did Eric think that Whalen could get Eric in trouble or that this had gone on too long or that Eric didn't know how to get out of it, or maybe Whalen had seen Eric, but maybe Whalen didn't know that he saw Eric?"

At that, Mountain turned and looked at her sharply.

She shrugged. "I was out there today, and I was looking intently all around, and my gaze kept coming back to that one spot. But what if Whalen had seen something like that and then, instead of checking it out, had dismissed it? And what if Eric had seen Whalen and recognized him?"

"The seeing is possible. Recognized? I don't know," Mountain admitted, "because that's not easy to do with all the outerwear we put on."

"And yet you all know how easy it is to recognize people just by their movements," she pointed out, "so, if it's somebody he knew and had worked with here or had gone on missions with… I don't think it would have been all that hard to ID one of us."

"That's definitely one angle, and we can talk to Whalen about that," Mountain noted. "He's feeling pretty much back to normal now."

"And Chrissy is obviously okay, as she made lava cake today," Emily said, with a big smile, "and, man, is it good."

Mountain stared at her in confusion.

"*Lava cake*, this chocolate cake with hot fudge pudding all through it," she described, as if Mountain were from another planet to not know this. "God, it was good too." She looked back at Nikolai, who immediately nodded in agreement.

Nikolai added, "Maybe she's like my mother, and she bakes when she's stressed."

"If that were the case with your mother," Mountain noted, "you must have done well growing up."

Nikolai laughed. "I did—in terms of baking, that is—but the reason she was so stressed was because my father was killed, murdered, in fact."

At that, Mountain stared at him. "Is any of that related to this?"

Confused, Nikolai shook his head. "I don't know how it could be."

"Did you know Eric back then?"

"Eric was from the same area of town, but I don't know that he would have known anything about it. I doubt it."

"Was he older or younger than you?"

"Older, but not by much."

"So, it's possible," Mountain stated.

"I don't know why it would be possible or what that would have to do with anything."

"On the off chance that it is somehow connected," Emily suggested, staring at Nikolai, "has there been anybody else here at the base who's from that same area, who might know anything about it?"

Confused, his gaze went from one to the other, as he tried to sort through what she was suggesting. "It was a long time ago."

"How old were you?"

"Thirteen," he replied, still frowning over her question.

"So, Eric would have been what? ... Fourteen, fifteen, maybe?"

He nodded.

"Anybody else from that region stand out to you now?" Mountain asked.

He shook his head. "A military base was close by, though," he mentioned cautiously. "So, adults only in that age group. Yet I don't know of anybody here now who would have been stationed there years before, but it's possible, I suppose." He frowned from one to the other. "I don't know that it's even possible to check something like that so far back."

"It's hard to say," Mountain replied. "I might have somebody I can call on about it."

"If it's Mason," Nikolai noted, "I've already contacted him." Mountain's gaze slanted in his direction. Nikolai shrugged. "I met him several times on missions, and, when I realized that I could be in trouble here, I contacted him for help."

"What kind of help?"

"Help in getting me out of this because I didn't do anything, and I don't know anything, but it feels as if I'm supposed to," he stated in frustration. "All I can tell you is that, if I knew anything, I would tell you."

"The problem is," Mountain shared, "there's a possibility that you *do* know something, but you just don't know *what* you know."

"Which then means Nikolai *can't* help because, if you don't know *what* you don't know," Emily explained, "then how can you help?"

"Of course," Mountain agreed, "but, given the level of

craziness right now, we may have to go through everything that Nikolai went through with Eric, conversation by conversation, as much as you can remember, to see if anything was brought up."

Nikolai's expression suddenly changed.

"What?" Mountain asked.

"One time he made a reference to old times, and I didn't understand, and he laughed and said, *You didn't understand because you don't know all of it, but no point in telling you. You were too young.*" At that, he stiffened and looked at the other two. "Surely he wasn't talking about my father?"

"I don't know," Mountain admitted. "It's a leap."

"Surely we can't afford to go down these rabbit trails," Nikolai offered, "when we're so low on manpower, especially if we don't know for sure that we're heading in the right direction. I honestly can't see how my father's death could have anything to do with this."

"How did he die?" Mountain asked.

Nikolai swallowed, hard. "As I mentioned, he was murdered."

"How?" Mountain pressed.

He looked over at Emily. "War games. As I can recall, we were told that he was in the wrong place at the wrong time, and he got taken out."

"*Great*," Mountain muttered, "so that brings us back to more military deaths."

"And yet he was a civilian," Nikolai pointed out.

"Sure, but he died as a result of military action."

"My mother got an apology for it," Nikolai related bitterly. "Not that it helped put food on our table."

"Of course not," Mountain said. "I'm sorry. It sounds as if you got the shitty end of that deal."

"The person who got the shitty end was my father," Nikolai corrected, his gaze hard on Mountain.

"Okay, I want you to take a pad of paper, and I want you to sit and to think hard. I want you to go day by day, conversation by conversation, training by training, and you can get the schedule from the day sergeant if needed. I want every conversation with Eric that you can remember, odd, normal, discardable," Mountain stated. "All of it. I want to see what might pop up as something out of the ordinary."

"A lot of it was out of the ordinary," Nikolai noted, miserable at the prospect of having to go through it all over again. "That's what I mean. Though I didn't really recognize who I was with Eric anymore."

"And that's what I need to know. So instead of taking this as if we are looking at somebody who you were great friends with and knew well, let's go back to the beginning, and look at this as somebody you didn't know at all and only first met here. Then take a look at those conversations with Eric from that viewpoint."

It sounded like a waste of time, but Nikolai could see that both Mountain and Emily were on board with that. Nikolai's shoulders sagged, as he nodded. "Fine, but we'll have trouble sorting it out."

"It doesn't matter," Emily argued. "You can do this. *We* can do this."

With that, Mountain turned on his heels and left, leaving them both to sort out the mess that was Nikolai's life.

DAY 3 EARLY MORNING

EMILY HAD STAYED up with Nikolai, going over everything that he had done with Eric while here on this base, which was shockingly little.

Nikolai looked at the pad of paper, where she'd been writing down the notes. "It doesn't sound like much, does it?" he asked.

"No," she agreed. "However, it does seem that you're remembering Eric as he was in the past, not as he was here."

Nikolai nodded slowly at that. "Nothing quite like realizing just how much you didn't know somebody."

"Even the idea that your father's death could have had something to do with this is mind-blowing."

"I doubt it's connected. Eric was cocky, as if he had some big deal going on here," Nikolai noted, staring off in the distance. "I have no idea what that *big deal* could possibly have been."

"And because he may have had a *big deal* doesn't mean it was a big deal that you could have done anything about," she reminded him.

He sighed. "Look. You're almost dead asleep, so go to bed, and we'll talk in the morning."

THE NEXT MORNING, Emily woke and stretched, feeling an odd soreness in her system. And now it was morning … and the last thing she wanted to do was roll out of bed. Even as she lay here, she heard the wind howling outside; the predatory storms seemed to be the norm right now. But she got up and got dressed. By the time she made her sleepy way into the kitchen, Chrissy was busy pulling out a pan of hot cinnamon buns.

Emily's eyes widened as she stared in delight at the treat, and then asked Chrissy, "Are you trying to make us fat?"

Chrissy laughed. "No," she declared, with a grin on her face. "It's just been a stressful couple days, and I absolutely love to bake, especially when I get upset and stressed out." She rolled her eyes. "So, you guys get the benefit."

"Oh, I'm not complaining." Emily smiled. "That's something Nikolai shared that his mom used to do."

Chrissy looked at her. "Really?"

She nodded. "Yeah, apparently, whenever his mom got upset, she would bake up a storm, so he was the beneficiary in that case."

"I can understand that," Chrissy declared. "It's a hell of an outlet. It certainly makes me happy and gives other people something to be happy about too. So, I can't see anything wrong with it," she murmured, "depending on supplies." She glanced back at Chef Elijah, who was behind her. "At the moment, we have a slight problem about disproportionate foodstuffs for desserts versus actual meals."

"I'm pretty sure the guys here would be totally okay having cinnamon rolls for their breakfast," Emily suggested, with a laugh.

"Maybe, but if they're doing any physical work today, the sugar won't hold them for long."

"It will hold them long enough to get back inside and to get the next meal though," Emily noted, as she scooped up a hot cinnamon bun and took it to a table. As she sat down, she watched Nikolai approach, with a cinnamon bun in his hand.

He shared, "I've never really been much into sweets as an adult, but this trip is changing me."

"How can you not be into sweets?" Emily asked, with a laugh. "They're not only delicious but everything is so gorgeous. Look at this. It's beautiful."

"It is, and they're doing a great job keeping everybody's morale up as best they can." He lowered his voice and added, "I thought of something else that Eric mentioned."

"Good," she said. "What?"

He shrugged. "Something about *payback*."

At that, she stiffened and looked over at him. "Any chance he was blackmailing somebody or maybe taking somebody else out?"

"I don't know," Nikolai grumbled. "I've been thinking of nothing else since I woke up with that memory."

"We'll have to go back over the notes we compiled last night and see if something else pops up," she added.

He rolled his eyes at her. "That big happy, positive optimism again."

"Absolutely," she declared. "And you, sir, are changing. You're not anywhere near as dour and dark and dreary as you have been these last few weeks." He made a face at her, and she burst out laughing. "See? That's much better."

"No, it's not much better," he argued, yet chuckled. "However, you are hard to stay mad at."

"Good, because I have no intention of letting you be mad at me for long. Why would you? I'm a nice person."

"You are," he confirmed. However, a cloud crossed his face again. "Sometimes I worry that you're too innocent."

"Ah, yes, innocence and all that good stuff. That may be, but I'm no fool, and I have a pretty-good grasp on humanity."

"Maybe so, but it's also easy to get caught up in the negativity."

"Not if you go with my attitude," she countered cheerfully, and then she stuffed a big piece of cinnamon bun in her mouth and crooned in apparent ecstasy. She looked at him in time to see an intense heat sparkling through his gaze. She flushed. "That apparently got your attention."

He shook his head, as if trying to forcibly will his own emotions back under control. "The look in your eyes," he murmured ever-so-softly. "I was wondering what it would take to put that look there myself."

"Yeah, well," she replied in a cheeky tone, "it's up to you to figure that out for yourself." His eyes widened but only for a moment, as somebody cleared his throat right next to them.

"I hate to interrupt," Magnus said, but his gaze held a knowing twinkle.

She smirked at him. "I do not believe that for an instant," she replied. "I personally think you probably live for moments like that. What with that pretty little doctor ..."

Astonished, he looked at her to see if she was serious and then started to laugh. "You certainly do liven things up a little bit," he admitted.

"Somebody has to," she stated. "The place is positively a downer otherwise."

"It wasn't always," Magnus clarified. "People have managed to do just fine here."

"Sure." Emily shrugged. "Some people were probably silently struggling."

He nodded. "I think that's something we might see a lot of in these scenarios, if we took the time to look for it." Then, as if shaking that off and changing gears, he sat beside them and looked around, carefully ensuring they were not overheard. "So, I understand Mountain gave you a job last night."

"Yes, and Nikolai thought of something that we didn't get on paper last night," she murmured. "Something that may or may not prove to be important."

At that, he looked over at Nikolai. "What's that?"

"Something about *payback* and *revenge best served cold* and *never thinking he could ever get away with this much*," Nikolai shared, as he stared off in the distance, concentrating. "A weird conversation, but Eric wouldn't clarify."

"No, but after having mentioned that much," Emily noted, looking at Nikolai, "any clarification would have left him too exposed, so he wouldn't have taken that chance."

⊕

NIKOLAI FOCUSED ON Emily, and then he slowly nodded. "It's almost as if you knew him."

"I did, though distantly at best, but I also knew that he was no friend of mine, and, if I were anything more, it would be disrespectful. So suffice it to say that I didn't like him."

"You and Teegan… you were close?" Nikolai asked out of the blue.

She frowned at him. "Yes, sort of. But again we were just friends."

"What did he make of Eric?"

"Teegan … wasn't a fan. We did have a conversation or two about Eric, just surface stuff, and Teegan warned me at one point in time to stay clear of Eric."

Nikolai stared at her. "Seriously?"

She nodded. "Yeah, seriously."

"That does give us a little more to go on," Magnus noted.

"Not really," she countered, as she looked over at him. "Everything we have is basically nothing."

"I understand, but all these individual bits will come together, and something will give us clarity soon," Magnus said, with a somewhat confident look on his face. "The guys went through the belongings we found."

"I would like to see those too," Nikolai noted earnestly.

Magnus looked at him for a moment, as if thinking it through. "That's probably a good idea. Everything is in his room and locked up. I'll take you there after breakfast." He looked over at Emily. "What are you doing after this?"

"I'm supposed to go help Joe today," she replied, "but I would like to come along and see what was found at Eric's campsite as well."

Her attitude made him laugh. "Sorry, that's not happening," he pointed out and looked at her sternly, "but I can understand how curiosity might be killing the cat now."

She nodded and gave him a mock glare. "And this one can get kind of nasty if she doesn't get her curiosity satisfied."

Magnus shook his head. "I never give in to blackmail."

At that, Nikolai stiffened, as if someone had pinched him. "That was something else that came up, and I'm wondering if Eric was involved in it somehow. Blackmail, I mean."

Magnus stared at him, clearly stunned. "Wow, well, we really need to talk then."

"I don't even have a whole lot to tell you, but, if it's possible, if Eric was somehow involved in something like that here, he wouldn't show any mercy," Nikolai commented, shaking his head. "That's the thing to keep in mind. He would show zero mercy to anybody trying to stop his plans."

"And so, my next question is, how was he doing for money?"

"I would have thought he was doing fine," Nikolai replied, with a shrug, "but he did tell me once that he'd lost a lot to gambling and was looking for a score to get out permanently."

"That will end up being one of the final pieces to the puzzle," Magnus stated, as he stared at Nikolai. "When it comes to money, people will do all kinds of shitty things."

"Yeah, but I never thought Eric would stoop to this kind of shitty."

DAY 3 AFTER BREAKFAST

AS SOON AS they finished breakfast, which happened at a fairly rapid rate given the conversation, Nikolai and Emily walked to meet Magnus at Eric's room. Just as they went to step inside, Mountain stepped out.

He looked at Nikolai, and then saw Emily behind him. "I wanted to come talk to you after this anyway. Come on in, and let's have a look at what was here." Mountain frowned at Emily as she tried to get in. When he held up a hand, she shrugged.

"I think I need to see it too."

"Why is that?" Mountain asked, as she stepped forward.

"It's hard to explain, but, more or less, somehow I think I'm helping Nikolai to trigger stuff, and that's bringing up more information." She was determined, and effectively in Mountain's face, or as much as she could be, given their size difference.

Nikolai spoke from inside the room. "She's right. She's helped quite a bit," he admitted. "So maybe you should let her come in and take a look."

At that, Mountain stepped aside and let her in. As she got closer, she eyed the selection of items on the bed and frowned. "An interesting collection," she muttered.

"Maybe, but what does it mean to you?" Nikolai asked.

"We've got survival needs. We've got ..." She turned

back to Mountain. "Did Eric have a phone on him?"

He nodded. "He did, but it's encrypted."

"Ah, so nobody here can break into it?"

"We have someone," Mountain replied, with a note of amusement. "He's working on it. He hasn't got through it yet."

"Ah." She nodded. "I figured somebody here would have that skill."

"There is, but it's taking a minute to break in because that phone could be huge. Besides, that is our one and only lead, so we are being extremely cautious, trying to gain access to that info."

"Given Eric's history, the psycho may have rigged it," Emily suggested.

"That could be," Mountain confirmed, "and it could also be nothing. Still we can't count on anything until we get in there."

She didn't say anything to that but watched as Nikolai slowly searched through the clothing and the personal belongings. "Is there anything here that Eric *didn't* have also at the base? Were you ever in this room, Nikolai?"

"No, I never was. I stood in the open doorway a couple times," he replied, still looking at the assortment of items. "I didn't see most of this though. I'm not surprised, but it does look to be fairly consistent with what I have known him to carry in the past. I'm not sure what it really means though. Nothing extra is here, if that's what you're thinking."

"That's exactly what I'm thinking. When you say *extra*, what do you mean by that?"

"I mean"—he stopped, looked around, and shrugged. "Nothing here shows communication with another party, no letters, no clues." He frowned and shook his head. "These items don't reveal anything really, do they?"

"That's what we were hoping you could tell us."

"Not yet," Nikolai muttered. "I don't have a thing to make of this—which would be Eric's intent." He sat on the bed and picked up the jacket Eric had worn and searched all the pockets and the inside lining. When he got to the name on the label at the neckline, he froze and stared at it, his body language alerting the others. "That's … that's not his name on this jacket," Nikolai noted.

"I recognized that earlier. Is it a Russian name?" Emily asked him.

"It's a Russian name," he confirmed, "but it's also …"

"What?" Mountain asked softly. "Who's name?"

"My father's."

Emily immediately walked over and sat beside him, hearing the devastation in his voice. "When you say it's your father's name, is that a common name?"

He looked at her blankly, and then his vision cleared slightly, and he nodded. "Yes, it's Peter here. Pete, Pedro."

"Right, so it's a fairly common name and doesn't necessarily mean anything at this point," she pointed out carefully.

He looked at her and nodded. "Right."

"Let's keep focusing and see what else we've got going on here."

He went through the rest of the clothing but kept the jacket off to the side. When he went through everything else, he looked to Mountain. "There should be more than a phone. He had a laptop and some electronics that he utilized here, and I did see them in this room before," he stated, looking around.

"Where would they have gone?"

"If Eric had a partner, I suppose they would be with

him," Nikolai suggested. "If there was no partner, then it's hard to say. Maybe he stashed them somewhere. In that case, they could even be on the base. He wouldn't really come to the base though if …" He frowned. "What if he …"

"Right or wrong, spit it out," Mountain said.

"What if he needed the internet?" Emily replied immediately, picking up on Nikolai's thinking. "What if Eric needed to send a message or to get a message or to contact somebody in some way? If his phone wasn't working out there in the tundra—which is a likely scenario, given the storms we've had—chances are Eric was coming here for that purpose."

"That's possible."

"What if somebody saw him? What if part of it all is the fact that somebody accidentally saw him?"

Mountain nodded. "That keeps coming up, so I've got to wonder. I think it's possible. I'll go talk to Whalen and get his take on it," Mountain announced.

"You can leave us here, while you go see what he's got to say," Emily declared.

He gave her a crooked smile. "That almost seemed to be an order."

She looked at him and shrugged. "It wasn't an order. More of … a comment. I think Nikolai could benefit from some time to sit here and process."

Mountain frowned, as Nikolai smiled at him. "I'm fine, but she's right. I do want to sit here and think a few things through. Some conversations I had with Eric didn't make a whole lot of sense. Yet, after talking about my father last night, then seeing my father's name here," Nikolai shared, "it's triggering all kinds of things, but I'm not sure what it means."

"You sit here and think about it then," Mountain stated. "I'll go talk to Whalen and be back in half an hour or so." With a hard look at Emily, he turned and walked out.

NIKOLAI SAT ON Eric's bed beside Emily, wrapped an arm around her, and gently pulled her into his arms. "I'm okay," he told her. "You don't have to defend me."

She shifted back so she could look at him, and an impish grin peeked out. "Are you sure? I feel as if the role is rather new to you."

"It's very new, and I don't wear it well," he muttered, "but I'm fine."

She laughed. "You want to be fine, but, given what you've been through, I'm not at all sure you could be. I wasn't trying to make you look weak or anything," she pointed out, with an eye roll. "I just thought you could use a few minutes to contemplate."

"Yeah, I'm working on that." Nikolai sighed. "I'm still dumbstruck at the idea that any of this could have something to do with my father." He gave her a kiss on the temple and then settled back against the headboard, not even catching the look on her face as he shifted. "The thing is, my father's death happened a long time ago, so how would Eric even have known?"

"He knew because it's part of his local history too, since you mentioned you two grew up in the same town," she noted. "But did he know anybody who was involved? Did Eric ever do any research during the time that he was here on this base?"

"*Hmm.* Yes, now that you mention it. I did ask him one

time what he was doing, and *researching* was his answer, but he gave me a halfway laughing look. When I asked what there was to research, he said something about his life after this."

"Right, so that could be his plans for his life, when he got a whole pot of money, could be what he was doing with his life here, or could be the life he would have after this because of what he was doing here."

"I didn't even consider any real answers at the time," Nikolai admitted, thinking back. "I laughed it off, as I do everything."

"And, if that's the way Eric expected you to take it, he was probably telling you the truth. You do realize that, right?"

"Yeah, I can see now that he probably was, but I don't know the topic of his research."

"I can't help but wonder about the phone that they found on him."

"Yeah, I'm sure whoever Mountain and Magnus have working on getting through the encryption is probably under the gun to get it finished. Hopefully they can recover everything Eric was doing."

"That could give us some answers."

"It might, but I still don't see how my father's death could have had anything to do with this."

"It depends," Emily added, with hesitation. "Maybe Eric found out about somebody who was related to whatever happened to your dad. Maybe Eric was putting the heat on someone and wanted money to keep quiet about it."

"So, what are you saying? That whoever killed my father is on this base?" He shook his head. "That won't wash."

"The only people here who are old enough to know anything about your father's death would be who?" She stopped for a moment and then answered her own question. "Chef Elijah, the colonel, and Joe?"

He nodded. "Three pretty stand-up guys in my book."

"Sure, but times haven't been easy on any of them all the time, so who knows? Maybe something from their past isn't so honorable," she suggested, then shook her head. "But still, that doesn't even seem feasible, does it?"

"No, and they're all American, not Russian," Nikolai stated, "and my father was killed outside of Siberia."

"I can't imagine what it was like, growing up there."

"Ah, it was fine." Nikolai waved his hand. "The thing is, that's what you're used to, and you don't know any different, so it's not some horrible place to grow up. It's just home." He smiled. "And I was well loved, which makes all the difference too."

"It does."

"It was hard after my father died, but I had some friends. When I say some, obviously Eric was part of that, but he wasn't a big part of my life back then. So, who is to say what happened back then?" He frowned. "It feels very wrong discussing Eric's world like this."

"Maybe so, but the investigators will do it anyway, so wouldn't you rather be at the forefront of it? And then, if you end up defending Eric, fine, as long as there's something good to defend," she stated. "However, if Eric was an asshole and was hurting people, then it'll be a little hard to maintain that position."

"He could have been an asshole," Nikolai agreed immediately. "And it's already apparent that he wasn't that good of a friend, so I don't know what I'm supposed to do with all that."

"You hold it close and keep in mind that he was who he was, and, until we know differently, he was a friend who you'd lost touch with," she stated. "We can't condemn him out of hand just because we don't know all that much about what he was up to. Yet he was obviously up to something, and I, for one, want very much to know what that was. Now, Mountain will be back here pretty-darn soon. You have anything else to add?"

"Not really," he said. "We've discussed the time when my father was killed, and I do remember when Eric was doing research here on the base, but he never really revealed …"

"Did he ever say anything about the CO? Did he say anything about people who were here?"

"Yeah, he told me that everyone was pretty well useless." Nikolai gave her a look. "And don't worry. He included you in that group."

"Of course. He was that kind of an asshole, wasn't he?"

"I won't argue with you there," Nikolai replied, chuckling lightly. "At the same time, he had no friends here."

"Which would be my next question. Could Eric have been friends with anybody here? Someone we don't really know?"

"Sure, that one kid. What was his name? Simon, Stephen, Spencer? Something like that. The one who defended Eric the other day."

"That is probably a case of adulation more than anything," she argued. "That kid is young and hasn't seen much or been in training very long, so I'm sure that somebody like Eric, who could do everything and could be everything to everyone, would look pretty appealing."

Nikolai gave her a quirky smile and nodded. "That is

exactly who he was, so you're right there." She nodded and didn't say a whole lot. He stared at the notepad in front of them. "I feel as if I'm missing something."

"In a way you might be, but let's not dwell on that and try to figure out if anything else comes to the fore instead. Is there anything else popping up or bothering you because that's what we need to know. We need anything and everything that could pertain to your father's death or to the life that you lived. And who would have been at that military base back then?"

"There were people from all over the globe, and I remember them saying that they had no way to prove who shot my father, but that it was friendly fire. Then they apologized to my mother."

"A nice thought, but I can't imagine a scenario where an apology would go over very well in that circumstance."

"No, she was pretty devastated. We both were, but never at any point in time did I contemplate vengeance," he shared, looking away.

"*Vengeance*," she repeated. "Did your father ever stray on your mother?"

Nikolai stared at her, immediately shaking his head. "No. Why would you even ask that?"

"I'm asking because I'm wondering if your father could have been Eric's father too." Nikolai stared at her and then sat back in shock, as she nodded. "Just a question, just thinking outside the box and all," she noted, carefully eyeing him.

"*Just a question?*" he grumbled, almost purple in the face. "Jesus, you're full of crazy questions."

"I'm asking them because they need to be asked," she stated, "and I get it. It's not anything you want to question or to even think about, but, considering that you were friends with Eric, that you were both from that time period, that Eric may have had something to do with all the deaths and accidents here and now, it's not such a far stretch to consider that Eric potentially may have had something to do with your father. So my question really isn't as crazy as it seems. So, could something along that line be possible? Is it possible that he could have been Eric's father too?"

"I don't think so," Nikolai said immediately.

"You don't need to answer right away. Take some time to stop and think about it," she explained. "I know you want to jump in there and to tell me that I'm off my rocker, but did Eric look anything like you and your father?"

He stared at her for a long hard moment, the color draining from his face. "You tell me."

She shrugged. "I don't know what your father looked like, so I can only compare you and Eric from weeks ago. It's pretty hard for me to tell now, but with the two of you growing up together, you probably would have noticed it more. Or, maybe not," she muttered, trailing off a bit. "Maybe you would have matured into it."

"I hope that you're wrong. … It would break my mother's heart if you aren't."

"Do you think it's possible?"

"Possible? Yeah, of course, because everything in life is possible. But probable? No. Hell no."

She smiled. "Good enough. I was hoping you would say that, but it's never that easy to understand when parents are having trouble, where that marital trouble comes from."

He winced. "There'll be a whole lot more questions like that, won't there?"

"Probably. Just think about it. A lot has been going

wrong here, and people must keep asking questions in order to get to the answers," she shared. "Nobody's trying to insult you. It happens to be a touchy topic."

"Yeah, you're not kidding," he muttered. "No, as far as I'm aware, that would not be possible."

"It would take DNA to figure it out at this point, I'm sure, and it's not as if we can do a quick DNA test here, but they might want to send away for it."

He stared at her and swallowed, and all he could manage to get out was a shaky mumble under his breath. When her gaze met his, he found his voice. "Fine. ... I would do it just to get it resolved. Again I would expect it to be a no."

"Since we don't know for sure, I highly suggest we get it done to get it resolved."

"Get what done?" Magnus asked, as he stood in the doorway.

She hesitated, looked over at Nikolai, and suggested, "You should tell him."

"She wants to know if, by any chance, Eric and I might be half brothers, and that potentially he was related to me through ... my father."

Magnus didn't appear to be surprised at that comment, or, if he was, he hid it well. "Do you think there's any chance of that?"

"I wouldn't have thought so, and I don't want to think it now." He raised both hands, shaking his head. "The reality of what I experienced with my family as a child has no bearing on what might have happened behind closed doors before I was even born."

"A DNA test would solve that pretty quickly," Magnus noted.

"That's what Emily said."

Magnus faced her and smiled. "It's good thinking. It's an easy-enough test to run, and I guess we can't exactly do it here, but we could arrange to get it done. But listen," he added, as he looked at Nikolai intently, "if and only if you're okay with doing that."

"Yeah, I'm okay with it," he replied reluctantly, an odd bit of fear in his posture all of a sudden. "But mostly because I'm pretty sure you're barking up the wrong tree."

"And, if we are, that's even better," she declared. "At least you'll know for sure, because if we don't do it now, that will rattle around in your brain forever."

"Because of you," he pointed out. Then he smiled. "I know you're trying to help, so don't mind my grouchy remarks, please."

"I am aware that I can be … hard to be around sometimes and that my attempts to help can come in a way that may feel as if it hurts far more than it helps," she admitted. "Particularly when the timing is urgent." She looked at Magnus and stated, "If it's related to his father's death all those years ago, this would be one avenue of exploration."

"Yes, but it's a good one, and one we can resolve with certainty," Magnus said. "Not too many people here are of an age that could have been involved."

"Which is why I brought up the half brother issue," she murmured. "Only three people here are old enough to have been at that Siberian base years ago. Unless of course somebody knew about it or in some way was affected, which could also be a family member of another generation," she suggested.

Magnus frowned and nodded. "We can have someone get into the research on that and see if we can track Eric's family back."

"Eric's mom is dead, and I don't think I ever heard about a father," Nikolai replied, immediately frowning.

"Was he close to your father?"

"I don't know that they were close," Nikolai said, staring off into the distance. "My father died when I was thirteen, and Eric was kind of around, but I didn't have any understanding as to what his role in all of it was. I just thought he was my friend. We were all buds in the area." Taking a deep breath, Nikolai continued, "You don't really know everybody, but you kind of do, and life happens so fast that you don't think about it."

"Now we need you to give it some serious thought," Magnus said.

"I have been thinking about it, and that lovely theory that Emily brought up is causing me to sit here and to ponder the rest of my life through a very different lens." He gave half a laugh and stood. In a slightly strangled tone, he added, "If nobody objects, I need to get outside and do something to clear my head from all this for a bit."

"Absolutely," Magnus agreed. He looked over at Emily. "You're slated to go help Joe today, right?"

"I am," she confirmed, as she got up. "I'm heading there now."

"Good," Magnus replied. "Getting away and clearing your head wouldn't be a bad idea either."

"Or"—she gave him a bright cheeky grin—"you're trying to get rid of me."

"No, I'm not, but clarity does help, and, besides, Joe is of the right age."

"I know," she stated, "as are Chef and the colonel."

Magnus winced at that. "You can bet that you won't be questioning him at all. He's already in the dog pile over all this mess at the base, doing what he can to keep his reputation and service record intact long enough to retire in good standing. So, do not in any way, shape, or form bring up this topic with the colonel."

"Of course not. I'll leave that to Mountain." Then she burst out laughing. "God help him if he asks those questions."

"Exactly, so off with you."

And, with that, Emily headed to the dog shed.

Magnus looked back at Nikolai. "Now, I need all the details about your childhood, as much as you can remember, at least."

"Can I get five minutes outside first?" he asked, looking at him warily.

Magnus nodded. "We're not the bad guys here, but you're the only source of information we have. So we'll keep coming back after the same issues time and time again, while we try to work out what happened."

"I get that, and I'm not against that. However, I am against finding out Eric was a sibling, and nobody ever told me. I was an only child and always wanted a brother or sister, but my mother would never talk to me about it."

"And this could potentially be why," Magnus pointed out. "It's one thing to find you have a sibling. It's another thing for your mother to learn that her husband had a love child, whether she knew about it or not."

"Right, and that's another part of this too," Nikolai muttered.

"Is she alive?" Magnus asked.

"She is, living in Germany now. I see her a couple times a year."

"What if you were to talk to her and asked her outright?"

Nikolai stared at him for a long moment. "That might be the best idea yet."

"Would she tell you?"

"I would hope so, given that I'm an adult now. However, this may have some implications that I don't really want to sort through." Nikolai scratched his jaw. "Still, I should give it a try right now."

"Maybe you should." Magnus eyed him closely. "And, if you don't mind, I'd like to stay close, so I could hear it too."

Nikolai groaned. "Am I under suspicion?"

"No, you're not," Magnus stated, "but something is seriously wrong here, and we don't want to let anybody else out of our sight, not until we have an idea of what's going on," he explained. "So, no, we're not watching you in order to keep an eye on you. We're watching you in order to keep an eye on you," he said, with a laugh. "There's a difference. Meaning that we want to keep you safe. You're the next connection to this mess."

"Why me?"

"Because, depending on what Eric was up to and who he was working for or against, someone might come to you next, either for information or to tie up loose ends."

DAY 3 MIDMORNING

OUTSIDE WITH JOE, Emily spent a few precious hours with the beloved dogs, laughing, talking, and visiting. Especially with Bertie. She took them all out for short walks around the compound. They had outdoor facilities as well as indoor, just because they were the kind of dogs that they were and absolutely loved to bury themselves in snow piles for a good sound sleep. When they were out there, they clearly slept better, deeper than any other animal she could possibly imagine. As it was, she was happy to get away from the base and the unanswered questions for a bit.

Joe commented on how stressed she looked. She smiled at him and nodded. "Yeah, somewhat," she stated, staring off into the white landscape, "but it's all good."

"Any progress?" he asked, his head tilting toward the complex.

She shook her head. "No, not really. More questions than answers."

He snorted at that. "That's probably a pretty standard protocol for anything that goes on out here," he noted. "One answer, two answers, and then it all blows up in your face again."

She smiled. "I've always been of the opinion that the answers should happen fairly easily." She snorted. "Instead they seem to be churning themselves all around, and we're not really getting clear-cut explanations on any of it."

"That's always the problem, is it not?" Joe chuckled lightly. "The elusive *why*, and, in this case, *Why would he stay out there alone?*"

"Here's one theory. It's been suggested that Eric was kind of egotistical and might have done it as a lark, maybe to prove to everybody that he could, so he could come back in with a big '*Ha-ha*, you idiots were all worried about me' attitude," she shared. "Personally that seems pretty farfetched for me, but I've certainly seen guys do plenty of stupid things."

Joe pondered that, as he studied the surroundings that he was quite comfortable in. "An interesting thought, I suppose. I didn't know the kid well, but I can't say I got along with him either."

She stared at Joe. "Really? And here I thought you got along with everyone."

"Nope, I sure don't," he declared, sounding bitter to boot. "And you're right. Eric was egotistical. Near as I could tell, he could do almost anything better than anybody else and made a point of making sure they all knew it. He didn't like taking orders, and he really didn't like being told he couldn't do something or have something. He was a spoiled kid, and, whenever you had to discipline him"—Joe smirked—"Eric wouldn't budge."

"Did you have to discipline him?" she asked in astonishment.

"I don't have to discipline anybody," Joe replied, followed by a laugh. "I just tell the bosses. Then they take care of it."

"Ouch. I bet that can make you pretty unpopular in a hurry."

"Sure, but I don't care," Joe stated, with a snarly expression. "I'm here to protect the dogs and to help educate the lot of you," he explained, with a hint of a smile. "Though some educate better than others."

"Some people just don't want to learn," she declared, sending a knowing look in his direction.

"They don't want to be told anything," he corrected. "That's part of it. Some people think they know everything, and Eric? He was a prime example of that."

"What about that Spencer guy?" she asked. "He seemed pretty big on defending Eric."

"Ha, he's fine. I've never had any problem with him, and he doesn't give me any lip. He's never given me any kind of argument, not like the rest of them do sometimes. But I'll tell you what, if it wasn't a well-run military outfit, no way I would have these guys around a lot of my animals. Some of their attitudes suck."

"Do you think it's just that they're not animal lovers, or is some other problem at the core?"

"I've assumed that they felt, with me being nonmilitary, that I shouldn't have the right to order them around," he suggested, with a grin. "Nothing quite like stomping on their egos a bit to make them all sit up and growl. They can do whatever the hell they want, but I won't have them near my dogs if those yahoos don't behave."

"Another difference here is, these are your dogs," she noted, as she looked around at the animals. "Fat and sassy, well cared for, and in great shape," she said, as she patted Bertie. "So you obviously look after them very well. I could see where anybody who doesn't look after their own as well might take offense."

"Maybe, though I think it's that whole ego attitude. A

lot of the guys come here because they think they've got it and know they can walk in and handle anything. But this weather doesn't necessarily allow you to handle anything, and it brings out fears that aren't always revealed in other training assignments or mental assessments," he explained, looking out to the vastness and back at her. "You don't think about what it's like to be alone up here for a long time period, until you are, and you find yourself cooped up with a group, while you're isolated from everybody else in the world—which is part of what this experience is all about."

"So, is that it?"

"Maybe. Although a few people have been livid because so many have wanted to leave and couldn't."

"Sure, but that applies to a lot of people, mostly because of all the shit going on," she replied.

Joe shook his head, then nodded. "And now we're left to wonder how much of that trouble was real and how much was Eric, just pulling shit over on everybody," Joe said in disgust. "With all the trouble he's caused, I could wring his neck myself."

She smiled. "I've already heard that sentiment a time or ten."

"Sure, and you'll hear it again," he stated, with a smile in her direction. "Look at the wasted resources, both human and animal, all put at risk out there searching for him, only to find out now that the whole time he was probably laughing at us?"

"Yeah, that's a problem everybody's having with this scenario, and nobody likes thinking Eric would do something like that. And, if they did get close to finding him out there, was it just competitiveness that kept him quiet? Or was it something deeper and darker?"

Joe eyed her sharply. "What do you mean by that?"

"I don't know for sure. It just seems odd. Why would he even do something like that? It makes you question his motives and his drive, and I guess that's the part I'm having trouble getting my head wrapped around."

Joe smirked at her. "Guys like that? They do it because they can," he declared, with a snort. "Sometimes you can make sense out of these guys, and sometimes you can't. I'm not saying they're all idiots by any means. I've met an awful lot of good people out here and a really good group is here right now, but you can also have a lot who think they're better than everybody else."

"That was Eric, apparently."

"Yeah, it sure was." Joe grimaced. "I had my share of arguments with him."

"Oh, I didn't realize," she said, a bit too quickly, earning a look from Joe.

"No, nobody did, and it's the kind of argument you have out here sometimes. The kind where something starts, and you aren't sure whether you'll get slugged or it will be a nothing scenario that ends as quickly as it started. Believe me. I would have taken the blow and made sure he got his ass kicked for it, but it never came to that."

"Did you ever tell anybody?"

"Nope, I sure didn't," he stated, "and don't you go telling anybody either."

She hesitated, then groaned. "Yeah, and yet, in telling me, you had to know that, under these circumstances? I don't really have much choice."

"Why not?" he asked, studying her, and then he glared at her. "Unless you're a spy of some kind."

She rolled her eyes. "Do I look like spy material?"

"Nope, but I've been fooled before."

Such an odd statement for him to make that she frowned. "It's just that they're asking everybody questions about any incidents with Eric, asking if they had any problems with him or heard him talk about anything, you know?"

He shrugged. "I'll have a talk with Magnus later—or Mountain. I'm not talking to anybody else though, and you better keep it to yourself. So, you can tell them to come talk to me, and that'll get you off the hook," he stated, with a gravelly tone. "Now beat it. It's got to be time for a cup of coffee for your sorry ass."

"I hope so," she muttered. "Yet all I seem to do is drink coffee nowadays."

"Make it something else then," he suggested, with a smile. "Be adventuresome. Pick out something completely different."

She laughed. "*Sure*," she quipped, with an eye roll. "What would that be? *Ooh*, how about tea? It's hardly a place to get adventurous."

"Ah, you'd be surprised." Joe chuckled. Yet, as she walked through the door, he barked out behind her, "Tell them to come fairly soon, in case I decide I don't want to talk."

"Will do."

And. with that she headed out. As soon as she got back to the main building, she tracked down Magnus and told him what Joe had said.

Magnus listened to her, frowning. "Why the hell didn't he say something? That old coot."

"I suspect he didn't want to be seen as weak or something," she suggested, "but honestly, the way he told it, I kind of got the impression that Eric may have really scared him."

Magnus frowned at that and nodded. "I'll go talk to him."

"You and Mountain are the only ones allowed to talk to him about this," she shared, "and he's not happy about even that. So go, but go easy on him."

"I will, and I know he's not involved in this mess. I've known him for a long time, and he really is a good guy."

"I won't argue that one," she replied, "although he kicked my butt that day, skiing with the dogs."

Magnus burst out laughing and quickly disappeared.

In the kitchen, she stared at the coffee and then at the options for tea, wondering if she really should try something different. The coffee was starting to … She wasn't sure if it was keeping her up at night, but the thought that it might be was enough to make her hesitate. As she pondered her options, Chrissy walked out of the back room and headed over to her.

"Hey, are you cold?" Chrissy asked.

"I'm doing okay," Emily said, "just looking at options for something to drink. I don't know why it's a hard decision today, but it seems to be."

She smiled. "You can get sick of the same thing after a while. So maybe a hot tea with lemon? I don't know, or even a broth, if you want some soup?"

"I'm not hungry though, but thank you."

As soon as Chrissy was gone, Emily quickly made herself a cup of tea. Studying it, as she walked back toward where Nikolai was, she wondered if she should have got him one too.

When he greeted her at his door, he asked, "Hey. You're

done out there with the dogs already?"

"I am for the moment," she said. "It's been an odd day."

"Yeah, for me too." He looked at the cup in her hand. "What are you drinking?"

"Tea of some kind," she muttered, with an eye roll. "I'm such a coffee drinker that I was trying to find something else to mix it up a bit."

"Well, you found it," he replied, as he watched her.

"Not sure if it's a good idea though." She grimaced. "And this is where you're supposed to be supportive and tell me it's a great idea."

"I'm not sure what rule book you're reading that from, but that might be a bit of a stretch for me."

At that, she laughed. "See? You're already starting to feel better."

He rolled his eyes. "Come on. I need to get something to drink too."

"Oh, *great*. So you'll have coffee, while I sit here and sip this concoction?"

"You can always dump it and get a cup of coffee," he suggested cheerfully.

"I suppose, though that seems wasteful, especially when supplies can be low. Did you guys get anywhere with all your talks?"

"I don't think so. Lots of supposition but absolutely no facts anywhere," he replied, with a sigh. "So, what am I supposed to say? One step forward and seventy-five back."

"Right, sounds about normal then."

"It does, and that's the problem." Nikolai grimaced. "No answers, lots of supposition, and some tangents now that are starting to get into the realm of strange. The minute my father got mentioned, everything felt bizarre to me."

"Hopefully the mess here at the base has absolutely nothing to do with him," she said, with a smile. "But, on the off chance that it does, you need to be prepared."

"I know it," he declared. "I do. And you're also the one who started that whole DNA testing idea, and now I can't stop thinking about it. I also tried to call my mom."

"Oh, good," she said. "I gather you didn't get through?"

"No, I didn't. I know Magnus tried a couple times as well, to no avail. I could try again now, but I know he wanted to listen in."

She winced at that. "Nothing like having conversations for everybody."

At that, Magnus came up behind him and offered, "I'm okay if Emily listens in instead of me, if you prefer, Nikolai. You just need somebody. If you want it to be Emily, that's fine." He looked over at her. "Are you okay with that?"

"Sure. I assume you just want a witness to it?"

"Exactly, and, if we can get some answers too, that would be even better," he noted, with a nod. "So, you may want to try again?"

With that, they took the tea back to his room, and he pulled out his phone and tried to get some reception.

When it went through, she was surprised to hear it buzzing.

He shrugged. "It did this before too, so best not get our hopes up."

"Right." But when a woman's voice came through the phone, Emily stared at him in shock. At least Nikolai was happy about that, suddenly grinning like a fool.

"Hello, Mom."

She gasped at the other end and cried out in joy. "Nikolai, what a surprise. Where are you?" He smiled, told her where he was, then the conversation turned to family, as they caught up for a few minutes.

Then, getting an eye from Emily, Nikolai took a deep breath and began, "Mom, do you remember Eric?"

Silence came first on the other end. "Yes. What about him?"

Nikolai hesitated, then said, "He's dead."

"Oh my," she replied in an odd tone. "Really?"

No sorrow was in her voice. He stared at the phone. "That wasn't the reaction I was expecting."

"I didn't know him all that well," she replied immediately.

Even Nikolai heard the dodge in her voice. "Okay, so … that's one of the reasons I'm calling," he added in a calm tone. "Do you … do you know who his father is?"

She gasped. "Why would you ask me that?"

"Because I need to know for sure. All kinds of issues surround Eric's death," Nikolai explained, trying to still the pounding of his own heart that was beating too loud in his ears, "and we're trying to get to the bottom of it."

"I presume he was killed in some unpleasant way," she replied in a hushed voice.

"He was killed while attacking a woman."

"Oh my," she muttered, and this time she did sound shocked.

"All I'm really asking for is the truth, please. It was all a long time ago, so if something is there that you think you should keep hidden from me, I would appreciate it if you didn't. I really need to know."

When she finally spoke, her voice was shaky. "It's very upsetting."

"I'm a big boy," Nikolai stated. "I'm sure I can handle it."

"Maybe you can, but I'm not sure about me. It *was* a long time ago."

"Okay, so let me ask you straight out as a way to start. Was his father my father?"

She started to cry, and he turned and looked at Emily. She shrugged and touched his shoulder in support.

"Yes, he was."

His mom was openly crying now, and he heard it all. "Why was it kept as a secret?" he asked, his surprise evident in his tone.

"What do you mean? It's not as if your father gave me much choice. He had an affair with Eric's mother that I knew nothing about, and he didn't find out about the boy right off the bat, but she did tell him not too long after the birth," she shared, between tears and sniffling. "He also had to keep paying for their care too, which made our life very difficult, and it was hard to forgive him for it."

"Of course," Nikolai added, wincing, "and you wouldn't have been terribly kind to her either, I presume."

"Why should I?" she snapped. "It's not as if I had a choice in how to handle this. Your father told me one night, after she had been making demands, and it made my life very, very difficult. Everybody knew except for me, it seemed. Neighbors, my friends, everyone. When I did find out, I realized it was common knowledge, and yet no one had told me. Even my own sister knew."

"I'm sorry. That must have been terrible for you."

"Absolutely humiliating," she snapped. "Why are you

asking about this now?"

"Because it came up with Eric's death," he replied, stifling an urge to lie.

"How could that possibly have come up?"

"There are some questions surrounding his death, involving potential blackmail or something else."

She snorted. "It wouldn't surprise me in the least. He came to me for money, you know."

"He what?" Nikolai asked in shock, staring at his phone.

"Yeah, he wanted me to give him money in order to *not* tell you."

He stared at the phone, incredulous. "I sure hope you didn't give it to him," he stated, with a flinty tone. "I am perfectly capable of handling the information, not to mention the fact that I've been an adult for a very long time."

"I didn't pay him," she declared, "but I did tell him what I thought of him. He laughed at me and said that he was out with you on lots of different missions, so he would tell you himself, whenever he felt like it. But he would choose the point in time. I tossed and turned about whether I should let you know, but it just never seemed to be the right time," she explained, "so, of course now, you're finding out from him after all."

"Not from him," Nikolai corrected, "but because of him, yes. I guess there is a bit of a resemblance that somebody noticed."

"There is no such thing," she snapped, followed by another sniff. "Absolutely nothing about you is similar to him at all."

"Mom—"

"No! Don't you dare let them goad you into believing it.

Whoever that was, they are definitely off their rocker."

He winced as he looked over at Emily, relieved to see a grin on her face. "Maybe so, but she was right though, wasn't she? Eric was my half brother."

Silence came again at the other end, and then her voice was suddenly weary. "I won't say I'm sorry that he's gone because he was a mean-spirited child. Still, he was your father's child, and that is something that would have upset him terribly."

"And yet Dad's also been gone a long time," Nikolai noted.

"I know. I know," she murmured.

"Was there anything suspicious about Dad's death?" he asked suddenly. "In the spirit of opening up communication here, was there anything about it all that bothered you or that didn't seem quite right?"

"You mean, outside of the fact that it was supposedly *friendly fire* and all the rest of that BS?" She snorted. "I don't know what happened." She took a deep breath and sighed on the other end of the line. "But honestly, trying to get any answers was like talking to a concrete wall. I couldn't get anyone to tell me anything. They gave us enough money to pay off the house, so I took it, and that was it."

"I didn't know that," he muttered.

"I guess there's some sort of beneficiary provision in a case like that," she replied in a meek voice. "Honestly I just looked at it as hush money, but I also was alone and had a child to raise. I don't even know what became of Eric's mother because she moved away when your father died. And, because she didn't have a legal child with him, she didn't get any of the support money either, and, no, I did *not* share," she snapped.

"I understand." Her tone revealed something else, and that did not go unnoticed.

"She was already a homewrecker, who had made a mockery of me. Your father was already giving her some money, so I wouldn't give Mia this money too. It was *our* money, yours and mine."

He winced at that. "That's good to know. Thank you for being honest."

"Yeah, *sure*," she muttered. "I still wouldn't have told you, if you hadn't brought it up."

"And that's wrong," he told her. "You should have told me."

"When? You idolized your father." She sniffled. "I wasn't … I never wanted to take that away from you."

"Yes, but I already knew that he wasn't a perfect man," Nikolai noted. "So anyway I just wanted to get some information and see how you were doing. I'm sorry that it's been an upsetting call."

"It *is* an upsetting call because of the terrible memories. But, like everything, it too shall pass." And, with that, they exchanged their goodbyes.

He sat here for a long time, staring at Emily. "I still don't understand how you knew."

She shrugged. "I could see it in a way, but I'm not saying that I really knew, not by any means. Just one of those things that I thought we needed to resolve, one way or another."

"I mean, this woman ended up having an affair with my father, close enough in time to father this child. But that doesn't mean that it *was* his child. I can see the potential of both his mother and Eric taking advantage of the unknown."

"Wow, you really don't like her either."

He hesitated. "Obviously it's making more sense now,

but she would never give me the time of day. That goes to prove that maybe she was his mistress for a time." Nikolai gave Emily a sheepish look. "I don't remember ever seeing them together, and she did have some other partners," he muttered. "So, I guess, for my own peace of mind—"

"We'll go forward with the DNA test then," she stated, with finality. "Let's get the truth out in the open for a change."

"Sounds good. ... I guess I need to go tell them."

"It would help, yes," she said. "At least then everybody has the same information, and maybe we can do something with it."

He smiled. "Come on. Let's go track somebody down." And they no sooner had started out of his room, when they saw Magnus walking toward them. As he got closer, Nikolai announced, "I got a hold of my mom."

"And?"

Nikolai nodded slowly. "Apparently Eric was my half brother. My mother is still pretty miffed about the whole thing," he added, with a half smile.

"Sure she is. People have these affairs on the spur of moment, and, when it spawns something much deeper, much longer, and much more permanent, like a child, the stories can get very confusing."

"If people would stop lying, it wouldn't be so bad," Nikolai muttered. "Anyway, I'm letting you know that I did talk to her, and, yes, it's confirmed somewhat, at least. My mother was told that my father was Eric's father, and my father was paying some child support to Eric's mother—who hated me, by the way. However, after my father died, apparently my mother received a settlement from the nearby base, enough to pay off the house. I don't know what the terms were, and she didn't say that she had to drop all the inquiries at that point in time, but she felt as if it were hush money. And, facing the reality of having a child to raise on her own, she took it and did not share it with Eric's mother."

"I'm sure she needed it, plus that would be her way of wielding some vengeance of her own." At that, Magnus turned to Emily and added, "So, good call on your point."

"Maybe," she conceded, "but also sad. Just think of Eric's attitude for all those years. I mean, Eric knew the truth and was waiting for the perfect moment to spring it on Nikolai." Then she frowned, thinking of something deeper. "You mentioned that his father took him out into the wilderness all the time?" she asked Nikolai.

"No, his grandfather," Nikolai clarified. "However, his mother had lots of men in her life, if I can put it that way. Yet his grandfather was pretty stable, and he was a really cool guy. But I wasn't allowed to go with them. I wasn't allowed to do very much with Eric or his grandfather. I guess I get it now, but I sure didn't back then."

"Yep, it messed up not just one life but multiple lives." She looked over at Magnus. "I still think… and Nikolai agrees, that we should get the DNA test done, just to confirm. If this Mia had lots of guys in the picture, there's always a chance that there wasn't that actual biological connection between Eric and Nikolai."

"No, I hear you there," Magnus replied. "I don't have a problem with getting it done, though it might be better to get it done stateside at this point, considering the logistical problems we have with transporting and testing."

"No, that's fine," Nikolai agreed. "It's already been however long, so a little bit later won't make much difference. And the fact that everybody believed it beforehand just gives us the information we needed for our purposes here."

"True enough," Magnus said. With a smile, he looked at both of them. "I talked to Joe, and everything's good there," he added, with a nod toward Emily. "You seem to be good at getting people to open up."

"Yeah, too good almost," Nikolai noted, with a chuckle. "I've talked to her way more in this short time than I've talked to anybody here."

"Yeah, you can't keep that crap bottled up," she muttered. When the bell went off for dinner, Magnus looked at them and shared, "I still have to talk to Mountain, so you may as well head on over to dinner. We'll join you guys later." And, with that, he quickly disappeared down the hallway.

She smiled as she walked toward the dining room with Nikolai. "Feel better?"

"No, worse, in a way," he admitted, glancing at her but smiling. "You find out the truth about your parents and your life in the most bizarre ways."

"I know," she agreed, "and, in this case, that really turned things upside down for you."

"It's just so strange to think that we were friends all these years—or at least I thought we were friends—and yet …"

"And yet maybe he was keeping an eye on you. You don't have to think of that as a negative thing."

He tossed her a sideways look. "*Really?*"

"No, you don't," she argued. "That could have just been him, not sure how to even have a younger sibling, and who knows? Maybe he didn't even know himself for a long time."

"I'm sure it wouldn't have helped his mom out to say anything about it. Yet maybe she expected my father to stay with her because she had a child, especially when I wasn't even born yet."

She nodded. "Maybe, and, as Magnus noted, lots of people get hurt by something like that." As they walked into the kitchen, they heard yelling. When they raced those last few steps to the kitchen, they saw a fire raging in the kitchen.

"Not again," Nikolai muttered, as he rushed ahead, stepping past Emily. Chrissy and Elijah were battling it quickly, but, even as Emily jumped forward to help, Nikolai grabbed a fire extinguisher and quickly put it out. When everything had calmed down, he turned and looked to see how bad the damage was. It had been fairly localized to the one area.

He looked around and saw Elijah standing there, glaring. "I know you probably didn't want me to use a fire extinguisher around food," Nikolai noted, his heart still racing. "However, in this case …"

Elijah nodded, still a bit sour. "It's fine," he grumbled, his hands on his hips, trying to catch his breath. "Dinner's already in the other oven, but this will be a hell of a mess to clean up." He groaned, pushed his chef's hat back off his head, and turned to look at Chrissy. "Did you see what happened?"

She shook her head. "Nope, I turned around and *boom*. Flames were everywhere."

Chef nodded. "We'll have a ton of people here and ready to eat in no time," he added, a bit calmer, maybe too calm. "You start working on dishing out the food, and I'll start cleaning this up."

Emily immediately offered, "Let me help too. Who knew a fire extinguisher made such a mess?"

"It does, but what else could you do?" Chef said.

And, with that, Emily and Nikolai pitched in to give

him a hand with the mess. As soon as they had things more or less under control, everybody filtered in for dinner. The first group stopped, took one look to the cooking area, and one of them muttered under their breath, "Again?"

"Yes, again," Elijah growled at them. "The food's out. Line yourselves up and eat."

"But is it even safe? Those chemicals are pretty poisonous."

Elijah shot daggers with his gaze.

"It's fine," Nikolai confirmed, stepping up. He pointed at the food on the other side. "Chow is out over there. We're still cleaning up this mess, so, unless you want to help, go grab your food and take a seat." Rather than helping, they quickly loaded their plates and sat on the far side of the room, where most of them ate and disappeared right afterward.

Chef shook his head. "What? Nobody wanted to help?"

"No, but at least you can cook on this other stove," Nikolai pointed out.

"Lucky I have more than one stove," Chef declared.

Nikolai asked, "But why was there a fire at all?"

"That's what I'm here to find out," Magnus announced, as he surveyed Emily and Nikolai, both in the middle of the way. "You two get into a lot of trouble, don't you?"

"Hey, that's not fair," Emily argued, as she turned from mopping up. "Besides, it's not as if anybody else was here to give a hand."

"No, it's true. They jumped in right away," Elijah confirmed in their defense. "We've got this pretty-well covered."

"If you say so," Magnus muttered, staring around in frustration. "It seems as if we're plagued with mishap after mishap." He looked over at the chef. "Any idea what this one was?"

"No, I don't," he replied, through gritted teeth. "Not yet, but I'll figure it out, once we get it cleaned up enough to see."

"I'll be back here after I've eaten," Magnus told him. "I've got a meeting with the boss."

"I've got his plate on the trolley over there," Chef muttered, pointing. "Take it with you and tell him we had another fire in the kitchen."

"Are you sure you want me to?"

Chef Elijah hesitated and then groaned. "Yeah, good point. Don't mention anything yet. Just tell him that I'm busy." And, with that, he sent Magnus off with the trolley.

It didn't take them very long to finish cleaning because the fire itself hadn't been very big, and only the one extinguisher had been used. At least it hadn't hit any of the food.

"We've got this part all cleaned up," Chef declared. "You two go on and get your dinner."

"What about you?" Emily asked Chef.

"I need this meal surface done, so I can put away the rest of the food," he explained.

"It really is safe to eat that, right?" she asked hesitantly, and he laughed.

"I'm not about to kill off everybody," Chef quipped, with a chuckle. "All the food was already over there. Besides, it's at the opposite end of the room. So, a little bit of smoke, and again, the food was covered, so don't worry about it. No chemicals, so you're fine." He shooed them both out. "Go on, go."

They quickly picked up their food and went out of the kitchen area to go sit down. "They used mostly water, wasn't it?"

"Yes, and that means it's fine. Besides, a little bit of char never hurt anyone."

She laughed. "I'm glad you said that because I'm starting to wonder about this place."

"You and me both," he agreed, with fatigue in his voice. And that was the last they said in the dining area, as they sat and looked around. Emily leaned over and asked in a whisper, "So, what the hell was that all about?"

He looked over at her with a hooded gaze and nodded. "I'm not sure," he murmured, "but I don't think it was an accident."

※

NIKOLAI DIDN'T KNOW what the hell that trouble in the kitchen was all about, but he was prepared to find out. As soon as he bid *Good night* to Emily, he searched for one of the other men working on the case. As soon as he saw Magnus, Samson at his side, Nikolai stopped them in the hallway and whispered, "What the hell is going on?"

Magnus returned a hard look. "We're not sure yet, but keep an eye on Emily, in case she's in the target zone."

"Why would she be?" he asked, surprised.

"Because I'm hearing rumors that she's affiliated with us," Magnus replied. "I can't stand that stupid *them versus us* crap."

"There shouldn't be a *them versus us*," Nikolai snapped. "We're all here on the same side."

"Have you felt everybody is on the same side for a while?" Magnus asked.

That stopped Nikolai in his tracks, and he slowly shook his head. "Maybe not."

"Exactly, and that *maybe not* is why you need to keep an eye on her."

He turned to look back in her general direction and announced, "She might not take it all that well."

Magnus laughed mightily. "Yeah, you probably got that right. And she could also decide that she should be looking after you."

"Me, why me?" he asked, frowning.

Magnus gave him a flat look. "Because of some rumbling that you and your buddy might have concocted something."

He winced and shook his head. "I can't say I'm surprised at them for thinking that. I guess I'm disappointed that that's where this is ending up."

"I'm not sure it's *ending* there at all," Magnus declared, giving him a hard look. "So don't go off and start doing something crazy. We need everybody on board and fairly calm at this point in time."

"Oh, I'm calm, provided everybody keeps their accusations to themselves." And, with that, he started to walk away.

Magnus called back softly and asked, "Hey, did you see anything, when you walked in on that earlier?"

He shook his head. "No, just Chef and Chrissy working on putting out the flames. We got there basically at the end of it."

"Was he upset?"

"He seemed more pissed than anything. I didn't get the details. I don't know if he's mad about the stove fire or something worse," Nikolai shared, "and Chef wasn't talking."

"I'll go talk to him," Magnus offered, "and we'll get to the bottom of this."

"If you say so," Nikolai replied. "I got the distinct impression that Chef was fairly unimpressed with the way things were going around here."

"I can't say that I blame him," Magnus admitted, as he eyed Nikolai. "Nobody wants to see this shit coming down, and that's not the first kitchen fire we've had."

"Maybe not, but if this is what's happening, maybe we're better off finding out answers, than sitting around, waiting."

"Oh, I agree with you there, 100 percent. The problem is, those answers aren't always that easy to come by." And, with that, he was gone, leaving Nikolai to stand in the hallway, wondering which direction he should go next.

Choosing safety for Emily, the one person who had stepped up to help him out, or at least to see if he was okay, Nikolai headed to her room. He couldn't do less by her. When he knocked on her door, she opened it and asked, "What's up?"

He looked around and then asked, "May I come in for a minute?"

"Sure." Surprised, she stepped back and let him in. "What's going on?"

"I was just told by Magnus that you need to be very careful. Apparently some more ugly rumblings are going on around here, and you've been slated as part of the investigative group now," Nikolai explained. "Of course I'm the target group."

She winced at that. "Sorry. I guess I'm not too bothered about being part of the investigative group," she muttered, with an eye roll. "But, Jesus, if people would just come together, we could solve this. Instead, everybody is choosing sides and looking at everybody else with suspicion."

"When it comes to survival, you've got to expect that," he pointed out, "and I'm not upset at anybody for having these kinds of thoughts. I just don't want to see it go so far that there's another kitchen fire."

Her eyes widened at that. "Do you think that's what happened?"

"I have no idea what happened," he admitted, shaking his head. "Magnus asked me, and I didn't have any answers for him."

"Yeah, but that's because we don't know anything. We got there at the end."

"And yet there was still food, and everybody in the kitchen was fine. Honestly, to me, Elijah looked more pissed off about the whole thing than anything else. He seemed more upset about the mess than anything else, which I understand, since he does have a distinctly ugly kitchen to put to rights."

"He also has people to help him clean, if he needs it," she noted, with a smile. "I feel sorry for Chrissy and Avalon and anybody else who's in the kitchen with him."

Nikolai explained more of what Magnus had shared, and she stared at him. "Right, so what do you want to do now?"

"Besides keeping an eye on you?" he asked, with a grin in her direction. "I think I'll make a quick trip out to check on Joe."

"Oh, that's a good idea." She frowned. "I can come too."

"No, don't worry about it," he said. "Let me go, and I'll be back in a few minutes. If I don't come back pretty quickly, you can raise the alarm." She looked at him worriedly and chewed her bottom lip. He reached out and tapped her gently on the cheek. "I'll be fine, but, given the circumstances, I want to make sure that Joe's okay too." She nodded and watched as he left.

He closed her door carefully behind him, and, moving

to his room, he layered up and headed out toward Joe. As soon as he walked in, Joe turned towards the noise.

"What the hell are you doing here?" he grumbled. "Or can't you live without your canine fix too?"

"Sorry, not trying to intrude on your personal space, and I know many of us come over to see the dogs. Still, it's hard not to, especially when some of us have pets and families we miss. So this, in a small way, helps us to deal with being away so long," he shared. "I have to admit to falling in love with Bertie …"

At hearing his name, Bertie came rushing over, a wiggling bundle of energetic fur. Nikolai laughed, as he crouched to cuddle the dog. "He's wonderful." He laughed as the dog wiggled and yipped and hip-checked him to the ground. Laughing, Nikolai grabbed and hugged the dog close, although that was almost impossible, given the wiggling animal.

When Bertie calmed down, Nikolai looked over at Joe. "Sorry for the interruption. I know you prefer your evenings alone. But not sorry because it does my heart good to spend time with these guys."

Joe shrugged. "It's just me and these guys anyway, so it's not as if I've got a hot date waiting for me," he joked, with a cackling laugh.

"Maybe not, but these dog are probably better company than a lot of dates."

At that, Joe burst out in a raucous laughter. "Oh, isn't that the truth?" He was all laughs. "I also don't have to follow the same rules that you guys do," he added, as he lifted up a glass that looked to hold whiskey.

"Ah, no wonder you're always so happy in the evening." Joe gave him a look, as he tossed back another sip.

"So, what the hell are you doing out here anyway?" he asked, taking a calm tone.

"Did you hear about the kitchen fire?"

At that, Joe lowered his glass and glared at him. "No, I didn't."

"I just wanted to give you a heads-up that another kitchen fire happened, with no obvious cause determined so far, at least not that I know about."

"Elijah would say it's an accident," he said immediately. "Even if it wasn't, he won't say anything different, but he would hunt it down himself though."

"You know him well, *huh*?"

"No, I really don't know him well," Joe clarified, "but I've certainly known him for a good many years, or at least been around him on occasion over a good many years. I've never had any problems with him, and I know he doesn't like it if anybody messes with his kitchen."

"Something I'm sure you can understand, given how you feel about your dogs."

"Yeah, and nobody messes with my dogs," he growled. "So that's why you're here, isn't it?"

Nikolai shrugged. "I just wanted to make sure you got a heads-up… in case this was something other than a simple accident."

Joe studied him for a long moment and nodded. "Okay, warning taken into consideration." Joe sighed. "If you hear of any other bad news, as much as I really don't want to hear it, do keep me in the loop, will you? And, if you hear about a fire, come over and check on us."

"Yeah, what is your escape strategy here?" Nikolai asked, as he looked around.

"The latches for the dog kennels are open all the time."

Joe pointed them out. "So, the dog can get outside as needed at any time, which is about the only good thing, considering how bad something here could go wrong," Joe noted. "Jesus, I really don't want to think about anybody going after the dogs."

"No, of course not," Nikolai agreed. "That would be horrific. And I think whatever is going on here is a human issue, and, as such, I don't think the dogs would be targeted, but the fact that they have their own way in and out does make me feel better," Nikolai admitted in a quiet voice.

"Yeah, me too," Joe murmured.

"Anyway, I'll head back."

"Thanks for the heads-up."

Nikolai headed back outside. It was cold, the wind biting, as he pulled up his collar and raced back to the compound and let himself inside. As soon as he closed the door, the wind ceased around him, making it almost calm, almost possible to hear again.

As he slowly took off his outerwear gear, he looked around to see that everything seemed to be here. However, with so many people on base, lots of hooks were in use. Hard to tell if anybody was out. Plus the base had no mandatory sign-in, sign-out sheet, with somebody policing it. Therefore, anybody could come and go.

Nikolai was still frowning, thinking about it, as he walked to Emily's room. When he got there, she opened the door right away with an audible sigh of relief. "There you are. Your last words were a little on the sketchy side as to the time to allow you, and, I have to admit, I was a little worried."

"I'm a little worried about *all* of it," Nikolai declared. "I'm so unsure of what to do, and I don't want to go in the wrong direction and get too spun up, especially if it's not needed."

"Exactly, but we also don't want to be too slack in reacting to all this and not have enough safeguards in place."

"I'm sure you'll feel better to know that, even if a fire happened at the dog barn, the dogs could get out just fine because of the way Joe's got the kennels set up."

"So, somebody would have to be intentionally trying to kill the dogs and must tamper with that setup in order to stop them from getting out."

"Exactly," Nikolai said.

"I can't imagine anybody here is particularly interested in that, but again … I guess we don't really know that," she admitted.

"No, we don't know that. If they can kill people left, right, and center… there's really no telling."

She frowned, nodded, and then settled back on her bed. "I've got a cup of tea and was trying to read a book," she mentioned, "but all these lovely intrusive thoughts keep getting in the way."

He winced. "Yeah, I've had more than a few nights like that myself," he shared, as he settled in the small chair beside her bed. "I should have gone and grabbed a cup of tea myself." He winced. "I'm still not quite used to that whole tea thing."

She grinned at him. "Coffee at this hour would kill me."

"Yet there have been more than a few nights where coffee at this hour literally kept me alive," he told her. "So, I will probably always prefer it."

"Sure, as long as it works that way for you. However, the minute you start getting balled up with too much adrenaline, you've got to cut that coffee out somehow."

He laughed at her. "Maybe."

"Go get yourself something then."

"Is the kitchen still open?"

"It was a few minutes ago," she said, "and, if it's not, it's probably just because of the fire. It might be a good time to go find out more about that," she suggested, looking at the door.

"You stay here," he replied, with a voice of warning. "I'll go take a look." When she glared at him, he smiled. "Ease up, will you? Nobody is making the suggestion that you're not completely capable of handling this yourself."

"Good, because I am, and I do have a fair bit of investigative experience. So nothing going on here would scare me away."

"Don't tell anybody else that," he pointed out. "Keeping that quiet is an advantage for you when we're in situations where … every advantage is helpful."

"I know," she admitted. "I'm just telling you. I haven't told anybody else."

He smiled. "And that's a vote of confidence I can get behind."

"You still haven't gone to get tea though, so maybe I'll come with you."

"No need." Nikolai held up his hand. "I'll be fine and will be back in a few minutes." And, with that, he closed her door and walked down the hallway.

DAY 3 EVENING

EMILY SIPPED HER tea, and tried to immerse herself in the book again, but couldn't. When Nikolai didn't return after ten minutes, she stared at her watch. When he didn't come back after twenty, she got worried.

Finally she dressed, adding another layer over her long johns, heading out to see what happened to him. She used the cup of tea as a guise, as she walked into the kitchen. Several men sat around the dining room in a group, but the conversation stopped as soon as she got there. She ignored them and headed over toward the teakettle, which she put on, and sat quietly, waiting.

She didn't bother them; they didn't bother her, and neither did they look her way, outside of that initial warning. And yet that initial warning was probably already enough to start whatever problem there was off again.

As she waited, she heard some of their conversations resume, but the discussion was very nonspecific, which she understood too. If she had been deemed as part of the enemy, that was their problem. She didn't have any enemy bones in her body, unless it was against injustices, and that was a whole different story. But the fact that she was also now friendly with Nikolai would only add to her isolation problem.

The reality that she would prefer to be a whole lot more

than friendly with him was something for her and her alone to sort out.

Maybe Nikolai too.

As soon as anybody else knew that she was heading in that direction romantically, it would change things again—and not in a good way. She never understood how you could wind up with a situation of *them or us*. And yet that's exactly what she felt she was up against.

She sympathized with the rest of the guys investigating here, trying to solve the problems because it seemed as if they were being blackballed just for doing their jobs. How did anybody get answers if you didn't ask questions? Particularly when so many people were intentionally hiding information. All it would take is a little bit of honesty to get this all solved. But everybody had secrets and things they didn't want to let out in the open, and, because of that, things would probably get dicey before they likely got any better.

As she looked around, she saw no sign of Chef Elijah or anybody else from the kitchen staff, but then it was already nine at night. Even inside it was cold. That same chill crept up on her too, but she knew that Nikolai had come in here, looking for tea. Yet she saw no sign of anybody in her group here now. She wondered if Nikolai had gone to bed without coming back and checking in on her, but that didn't make sense. He'd made it very clear that he would check in on her, if for no other reason than to stop her from worrying. Right now, *worrying* is exactly what she was doing. As she looked around at the dining room again, there was still no sign of him.

When she'd had enough of it, she walked over to the dining room table with people seated all around it. "Hey, have you guys seen Nikolai at all?"

Smothered grins came from several of them, but they all shook their heads.

"He came here to get a cup of tea, and yet I don't see him."

"I highly doubt he's too bothered about checking in," replied one of the men, with a snarky tone.

She looked at him intently and tried to remember his name. "I hardly think checking in is what I'm asking for," she declared, "but, hey, you take it any way you want." He glared at her, and she shrugged. "Honestly, with the number of accidents and injuries and disappearances around here, you would think that everybody would be on a buddy system."

One of the other men nodded. "I was wondering about that," he admitted, "because it's pretty-damn strange that we're having so much bad luck."

"I don't know about *bad luck*," argued one of the men in a hard voice. "Pretty-damn sure all of this luck is man-made, and that's an entirely different scenario."

She didn't say anything, but her teakettle whistled, which gave her a good excuse to head back over and to make a cup of tea on her own. As soon as she was done, she smiled at the guys and walked out, knowing that the conversation would immediately turn to her, as soon as she left.

She walked down the hallway and headed toward Nikolai's room. She got no answer when she knocked on the door. Worried now, she sent him a text, and, when he didn't respond, she kept walking to the medical center, wondering if Magnus would be there with Sydney. No reason for them still to be there, but also no reason for her not to hear back from Nikolai. She didn't make it that far, before she caught sight of Mountain.

He looked at her closely. "Not used to seeing you out and about so late."

"If I wasn't looking for Nikolai, I wouldn't be out right now either." Then she quickly explained what had happened and what he had said.

His gaze was intense as he studied her. "Do you think he would have stuck by that?"

"Absolutely," she stated. "He has never *not* stuck by it, at least in my experience to date."

He nodded. "He went to talk to Joe earlier. Do you think he went back out there again?"

She stared at him. "Oh, I never considered that." She turned toward the door.

"I'll go take a look," Mountain offered, holding up a hand to stop her from heading outside. "You go to your room and stay there, please, so we have some idea where you are."

"Right. The last thing we need is anybody else going missing."

He gave her a warm glance. "Exactly, and cooperation makes a big difference for everybody."

Sighing, she headed back to her quarters and waited. When Mountain came to her room a few minutes later, he had Magnus with him.

"He's not with Joe, and he hasn't been seen in the last little bit, so tell me exactly what he was doing." She explained that he would grab a cup of tea and check on the kitchen.

"Is it possible you two got your wires crossed, and maybe he just headed by to his room afterward?"

"I checked his room when I came back, since he wasn't in the kitchen. I thought maybe he'd gone there after all, and

I was okay with that. I just wanted to know that he was safe," she explained. "But, no, the plan was that he would come right back. Magnus had warned Nikolai that he should keep an eye on me. And he was." Nervously she shifted her cup from one hand to the other. It was still hot, and she needed the added warmth, as she stared at him. "Please tell me that Nikolai's not missing."

Magnus eyed her, his face grim, as he shared, "We're about to do a full-on check, so I'll let you know in a few minutes." As he went to leave, he turned to her again and said, "I would suggest that you stay here in your room. We can't have more people going missing." Almost numb, she nodded, and stayed exactly where she was, but it took them forever to update her.

When Magnus came back, some forty minutes later, his face was grim. "No sign of him."

She swallowed hard and whispered, "Is his jacket and everything here?"

He nodded. "Mountain has gone out to the generator and is checking the outbuildings and any other buildings, and for other tracks out there."

"*Right*," she muttered, with a nervous laugh.

"Had he come up with any earth-shattering answers?"

"No." She gave him a solemn nod. "At least I don't think so. He didn't tell me if he did, but I know he was quite concerned about all of this going on. When you told him to keep an eye on me, he really didn't like hearing the possibility that other people would get hurt. So I wouldn't be surprised if he was off, trying to find some answers."

"Which we're all trying to do," Magnus noted.

"Sure, but information isn't flowing that well, and I think he's getting frustrated and fed up. There's also that level of disconnect with everybody else around here, and I think he's afraid that I'll get tarred by the same guilty brush that he feels he's been tarred with. I don't think he particularly cares for himself, but he may be worried that I'll suffer for it."

Magnus immediately nodded at that. "I agree with him. You probably are, perhaps doubly so, since you're tainted both by your association with him and with us, which is one of the reasons why everybody is trying to make sure you stay where you are and stay safe."

She gave him a ghost of a smile. "That's nice, but no point in staying safe if Nikolai's gone off to try and solve a problem, and it's put him in more danger."

His phone rang then. "It's Mountain," he told her, as he quickly answered the phone and asked right off the bat, "Did you find him? … You did? Thank God for that." Then he frowned and nodded. "Yes, I'll get her. We'll meet you at the clinic." Then he hung up and looked over at Emily. "He was found in the generator shed at the back, under a bunch of tarps."

"Jesus Christ," she muttered, bolting to her feet and grabbing more clothes.

"You stay here," he said.

"The hell I will," she snapped. "In case you hadn't noticed, somebody's trying to kill him."

"Yeah, we noticed," Magnus declared, "and I'm heading down to give Sydney a heads-up."

"Right," Emily noted. "I'll meet you there." Within seconds Magnus was already striding down the hallway, shaking his head and mumbling to himself.

She quickly ran to the bathroom, her mind consumed with what could have gone wrong. By the time she reached the medical clinic, Mountain carried Nikolai, a large man in his own right, over his shoulder, his face grim.

He caught sight of her and frowned, but, as she jutted her chin out and glared at him, he nodded. "All right, but you stay quiet."

She nodded mutely and followed as he took Nikolai into the clinic.

※

NIKOLAI WOKE UP, his head pounding and a burning heat firing through his system. He groaned and shifted, trying to get away from it.

"Nope, don't fight it," said someone, pushing him down and holding him there. "I've got to get your core body temperature back up again."

Not sure who was talking or why, he opened his eyes, his eyesight struggling against the bright light. Almost immediately the light was dimmed, and he whispered, "Thank you." He wasn't sure who had done it, but it helped.

"At least he's talking."

Nikolai almost recognized the man's hard tone. Moments later, with his eyes still closed, he didn't need his vision to know Mountain's strong voice. Nikolai whispered, "What happened?"

"That's what we're waiting on you to tell us."

He slowly opened his eyes, then looked around and saw Emily right beside him. He reached out a hand. "Sorry. Guess I didn't make it back, *huh*?"

"No, you didn't." She glared at him. "You were supposed to be getting tea."

He frowned at her. "*Tea*?" He wasn't quite coherent,

and he knew that, as he struggled to put her words into context. "I don't drink tea."

"No, you don't normally, but you decided you would try some this time, instead of coffee, because you hadn't been sleeping well."

He blinked at her slowly. "And I didn't get tea?"

"If you did, you didn't come back with it, and, when you didn't return as promised, I went looking for you," she explained.

He groaned and shifted in the hospital bed, feeling his body burning up. "Christ, the heat."

"Yeah, well, when you're that cold, Sydney had to induce heat any way we can get it," Emily told him. "I'm not particularly happy with your temperature."

He was taking in the information but wasn't processing it well. His tongue felt thick, not moving properly, and even the words were hard to form.

"I know you're struggling, and that's all right. We're getting you warmed up, which will help. We were hoping that you could tell us what happened, and maybe who knocked you out," Emily explained, "and then Sydney can get these guys to leave."

Nikolai blinked several times, noting that Magnus was right here too. In the background, somebody else stood in the doorway. He tried to get his brain clear enough to provide some information.

Magnus stepped forward and asked, "Do you remember anything?"

Nikolai slowly shook his head. "No, not really. It's all a blur. Too much." His voice even now was having trouble getting any words out. He looked at Sydney, frowned, and managed to ask, "Drugs?"

She immediately came closer and checked his body for needle marks and, sure enough, found one on his neck. The others completely changed their quiet line of questioning around him, and each stepped closer to see it for themselves. He heard the anger rise in their voices, right before he closed his eyes, shaking not so much from the cold as from the actual injection. He lost consciousness, came back, lost consciousness, came back.

On the next round, Sydney looked at him and smiled. "Hey, glad to see you back again."

He stared at her and whispered, "Water?"

She immediately brought him a glass of water with a straw, and he slowly sipped at the water. Then he realized Emily was holding his other hand. She looked at him, tears in her eyes.

He whispered, "Not dead."

"Glad to hear that," she replied in a gentle voice. "You came to warn me about making sure I stayed safe, but I think you forgot to look after yourself."

He blinked at her several more times, his brain clearing, and he felt a whole lot more like himself. He squeezed her fingers and whispered, "Wasn't expecting it."

"No, and that seems to be the problem," she noted, with a flare of anger rising within her. "Nobody's expecting it, and people are getting completely sidelined. The question is, was it friend or foe?" Emily asked.

Nikolai wanted to say something smart because obviously it wasn't a friend and had to be foe, but she was right. Was this foe in disguise as a friend? He sucked back on more water, as he tried to process a little faster. When he finally could, he told her, "I don't remember anything. Not even getting the tea."

"Now that we know you've been drugged," Sydney noted from his side, "it's safe to say that you may not recover that information." She studied him and took his vitals again. "I want to get most of it cleared out of your system, especially since we don't know what it was."

Emily added, "It doesn't even make any sense that they would have drugged him. If the plan was to kill him, all they had to do was knock him out and leave him out there. He wouldn't have made it long in this weather, especially dressed as he was."

Sydney looked over at her and nodded, but the doc didn't say anything.

Nikolai hated to even hear such words, but Emily was right. He didn't know what had happened and didn't remember hearing anything. "Honestly, the last thing I can remember is walking toward the kitchen," he murmured.

"And the rest may or may not come back, so don't try to force it," Sydney warned him. "Give yourself a chance to heal and then we'll see how much of it comes back."

He stared at her. "It's got to come back. Otherwise it'll drive me nuts."

She smiled at him. "You aren't the first person to tell me that," she shared. "We'll give it some time and see how it goes. Don't worry. You're not going anywhere tonight, and, therefore, neither am I. So we can see how it goes."

At that, Emily looked over at her. "Do you always stay if you've got a patient?"

"Somebody will stay here for sure," she declared, with a smile. "I might switch it up with a couple of the other guys, depending on how Nikolai's doing."

"I'll stay," Emily offered immediately. Sydney hesitated and Emily shrugged. "I'm trustworthy, honest."

"It's not that, but if anything should go wrong …"

"Like what?" she asked, exasperation and frustration evident in her tone. "He's here now, and you're only what, next door?"

"Yes, I am exactly that, so it could work." Sydney stared at Nikolai. "What do you think about that?"

"I think Emily should go back to her room and stay where she's safe," Nikolai replied. "She shouldn't be risking her life here with me."

Emily snorted. "How is me being here, sleeping in a chair somewhere close to you, risking my life? Let's not get into histrionics."

He glared at her, but she was grinning at him. "How can anybody stay mad at you?" he asked.

"They can't," she stated cheerfully. "So, get over it already."

He shook his head. "You shouldn't even be involved."

"Let's not go there," she stated in a warning voice. "Remember who you're talking to."

He stared at her and slowly nodded. "Fine," he grumbled. Then he turned to Sydney. "Maybe people should be here in shifts."

"Oh, I'll figure it out," the doc said, "but let's see if we can get you fixed first." She was clearly not happy with his condition. "I'm not too thrilled at how you're doing at this point."

"Neither am I," Nikolai confirmed, as he settled back against the bed. "I'm not feeling what I would say is 100 percent."

"Of course not," Sydney replied, "but, if I could even get you back to say, 75 percent? I would feel a lot better."

"Do you really think somebody was trying to kill me?"

he asked.

"If they were, they went about it in a difficult way. As Emily pointed out, it doesn't take that much to kill somebody in these temperatures. It doesn't make sense that they drugged you *and* knocked you out. All they really had to do was one or the other. Then just leave you alone out there and let you die. But instead they did both. So, I'm not sure if that was in order to get you out of here and then left someplace to die or if they wanted something else from you."

"What could anybody want from me?" he asked, confused. "It doesn't make any sense."

"Keep in mind that, considering Eric had been living off base, it's possible that maybe he had a partner, and maybe that partner came back for you, just to find out what happened to Eric."

Nikolai's eyes widened at that. "Somebody *was* talking to me." He shifted in the hospital bed. Immediately Emily squeezed his hand. He looked at their laced fingers and smiled. "Outside the kitchen," he muttered. "I think somebody stopped to talk to me, and I'm not sure what happened after that."

"They probably wanted a closer talk than you were really looking for," Emily quipped, with a smile.

"Maybe, I don't know. I can't… I can't remember."

She nodded. "Remember what Sydney said about your memory."

"*Great*. If you guys have your way, I'll never find out."

"Of course you will," Emily argued, with a bright smile. "You just can't hurt yourself in the process." At that, the clinic door opened again, and Mountain walked in.

He looked at them all. "Well?"

Nikolai shook his head. "Memory's pretty spotty. All I

can remember at this point is meeting somebody in the hallway and feeling… feeling surprised because I didn't know who they were," he shared, after a moment. "At least I don't think I did."

Mountain stepped forward, his gaze sharp. "Meaning?"

"I don't know exactly." He wanted to backtrack but wasn't sure that he should. "The only thing I can tell you right now, given my spotty memory, is that it felt as if I didn't know who he was. So somebody new was on the compound that I hadn't been introduced to, didn't know, or something," he suggested. "The ladies here have suggested that maybe he was whoever Eric was working with—*if* Eric had a partner. That maybe he thought I would be the best source of information on what happened to Eric," he said.

Mountain immediately nodded. "That thought occurred to me too, and I'm checking all the cameras right now." Then his lips quirked, and he clarified, with a feral grin, "Well, Magnus and Egan are. They're looking to see if anybody else came in unexpectedly."

"It's pretty interesting that's even a possibility," Emily noted, off to his side. "We don't think of this as a place somebody wants to break into, not with all the shenanigans going on here."

"True," Mountain agreed. "In several cases, we've already had people looking to break out of the base, despite the dire weather consequences," he reminded her. "So, people will do what people will do. We just have to try to understand the reasons."

"I definitely don't understand this. Were you here when we confirmed Nikolai was drugged?" Emily asked Mountain.

At that, his gaze turned to Sydney, and she nodded. "She's right. I'm still getting his system cleaned out. I don't have any way to identify what that drug is right now, but Nikolai is cognizant and is improving, and I'm running a bunch of tests, hoping that it was a fairly minor dose of whatever."

"What good is a minor dose? Why even give it to him?" Emily asked.

"I know," Sydney muttered, "and that'll be something to deal with." The doc checked his blood pressure again. "His vitals are slowly getting back to normal," she murmured, "but I'll keep him here overnight."

"I'll stay," Emily stated. Mountain raised his eyebrows at her, and she glared at him. "Sydney can't stay up all night looking after him," she argued, rather fiercely, "so I'll split it with her."

He shrugged, as if it was nothing to him, which, in a way, it probably wasn't. Sydney had the right to make the calls in her clinic, and, if she declared that somebody should stand watch, then somebody would stand watch, and that was that.

Emily repeated, her stance defiantly, "I want to be here."

Nikolai squeezed her hand to calm her down. "It's all right. Mountain's not telling you … See? You can stay."

She laughed. "That's good." She sent a cheeky look in Mountain's direction. "Then we won't fight about it."

He looked at her in astonishment, then suddenly grinned. "That would last all of five minutes."

"You never know," she muttered.

He slowly shook his head.

Then separating herself from Nikolai, she stood to face Mountain. "I have no intention of fighting you. I just want to ensure Nikolai stays safe."

"Believe it or not," Mountain replied, with a note of

humor, "we want that to happen too."

As soon as Mountain left, Sydney looked over at Emily and said, "Look. I'll be here for a while yet, so why don't you go get whatever you need for the night, and then come on back. By then, I'll have him ready for bed."

Emily nodded and quickly took off, heading out of the clinic.

At that, Sydney turned to Nikolai. "If you seriously don't want her here, now would be the time to say so."

He stared at the doc and then smiled. "No, that's fine. Emily's fine. It'll be really nice to have her company," Nikolai replied. "I didn't want her to be put out though."

"She seems pretty interested in making sure you're okay."

"Which is kind of—" He stopped, then shrugged. "It's not exactly how I want to be seen, as somebody who needs a nursemaid," he muttered.

She snorted. "I don't think anybody here will make that mistake."

"If you're sure, I'm good with it. … I really like her."

"It appears that the feeling is mutual," Sydney confirmed, with a gentle smile. "Relationships at this place can be a little hard to make happen though."

"I don't quite understand that either," Nikolai admitted. "You would think there would be lots of opportunities for relationships."

"Sure, plenty of *opportunities*," Sydney noted, with a chuckle, "but do you really want a relationship based on opportunity or a relationship that's best for you?"

"One that's best for me," Nikolai stated immediately, "and, honest to God, I wasn't even thinking that a relationship was possible."

"No, of course not." The doc smiled. "You probably came here thinking it would be all war games, with no idea that a potential romance was possible."

"Never crossed my mind… and I sure never expected it to happen this way."

"I wouldn't worry about it right now. Just know that she's obviously interested." Sydney rolled her eyes. "And, putting in my two cents, anybody who volunteers to stay up all night to ensure you're okay has got to be good people."

"Unless she's trying to poison me or something," Nikolai teased, followed by a chuckle.

"If that's the case"—Sydney eyed him—"maybe I shouldn't have her stay over."

"No, no, don't do that. I was only joking."

"Not that funny under the circumstances."

"I know," he conceded, "but it helps to make light of the situation. It's a very awkward thing to realize that I was almost killed, taken out by somebody my mind is saying I didn't recognize. A stranger, which makes no sense, given where we are."

"Unless it happens to be a friend of Eric's."

Nikolai nodded. "Maybe that's all it was. Maybe that's all I'm thinking of. I don't know." He shook his head. "It's confusing and so frustrating because I want all the information in my brain to pop to the forefront and give me the answers I need," he grumbled. "Instead I'm getting no answers at all."

"The answers are there," she corrected, "and I suspect, by morning, you'll wake up and know exactly what you're trying too hard to remember right now."

He smiled. "I think you're being an optimist."

She chuckled. "Absolutely I'm an optimist. Trust me.

You have to be to live and work here," she declared, with a smirk. "Think about all the things that have gone wrong on a regular basis."

He winced. "Yeah, and I wasn't even thinking along those lines."

"Maybe don't think about it at all," she suggested, "because an awful lot of things in life can go wrong, without requiring any assistance from anybody." And, with that, she added, a warning in her tone, "Now get some rest. I'll go do some work at my desk. Whenever it's time, and I feel everything here is done the way I need it to be, I'll head off and grab a little sleep. Then I'll see you in a bit."

With that, she headed to her desk, and he realized that, for better or for worse, she was telling him to relax and to stop worrying.

Now if only that were easy to do. However, it wasn't long before he felt himself drifting off into a deep sleep.

DAY 3 NIGHT

WHEN EMILY KNOCKED gently on the clinic door, it opened immediately, startling her, and Sydney was there, holding the door for her.

"Sorry," the doc whispered. "He's dropped off to sleep, and I didn't want you waking him, so I've been waiting for you on this side of the door."

Emily winced at that. "Sorry, I would have been here sooner."

"No, no, it's fine," the doc said, her voice low. "I didn't want you knocking and have that wake him."

Emily walked over to take a closer look, and, indeed, Nikolai was sleeping, his chest rising and falling in a steady relaxed manner. She walked over to where Sydney sat now. "Is it okay if I lie down on the other bed?" Emily asked.

"Sure, and it's okay if you nod off," the doc added. "I'm pretty sure he'll sleep through the night now. If nothing else, those drugs will need an outlet."

"The thought that somebody even did that to him makes me sick." Emily shuddered.

"I know. It's terrible," Sydney agreed, getting up from her desk. "I'll head out now. Go ahead and lock the door behind me," she pointed out.

"Then how will you get in?" Emily asked, confused. "What if I fall asleep?"

"I have keys," she shared, looking at her with a smile. "So go ahead and sleep. It's not an issue."

"Won't that defeat the purpose of me being here?" Emily asked.

"I suspect you'll be tired enough that you drop off anyway."

"No, I won't because I won't allow myself," she declared, with a determined tone.

"Okay, good enough then." Sydney checked the clock and nodded. "It's amazing how time goes by when you're having fun." She gave a light chuckle. "I'll head off and get some sleep, and I'll see you in a little bit." And, with that, she walked out the door and closed it quietly behind her.

Emily walked over and quickly locked it. Even as she did so, she felt an eerie loneliness creeping up on her. Being here all alone in the clinic was giving her a weird vibe. Everybody else on the base was asleep or out of commission, one way or another, and she was all alone in this eerie silence.

A career in the military hadn't exactly been something she had ever planned on doing, yet it felt right from the minute she'd joined up. But now, being here and dealing with all this, lent a completely different meaning to the work that she did. Adrenaline had kept her up so far, but now she felt the full blast of what was happening all around her. Everybody here was as skilled as she was, if not way more. Some of the people here had years and years of experience. However, she had to remember that, just because she might feel as if she wasn't as good as some of them, that didn't mean it was true. Plus, right now, the job of looking after Nikolai was something she planned on taking very seriously.

She had brought a book and her laptop, and she also had her phone fully charged, so she should be fine. And, with that, she settled in for a good night, with the book she had brought. When an odd sound came about two hours later, she stood and looked at the door warily. Only Sydney had a key. Emily quietly walked over to the door and watched as somebody twisted the knob.

She hesitated, wondering if she should open it and go after whoever it was, but cameras were outside, and whoever was monitoring it could check. She quickly pulled out her phone, and, keeping it on Mute, texted Mountain that somebody was trying to get into the medical center, where she was locked inside with Nikolai.

His response was immediate. **Stay there. Stay locked up.**

She then assumed that he was on his way down the hallway to come check on her. She heard voices a moment later and a shout at somebody outside. She then heard someone running, racing along the hallway. Mountain knocked on the door a little later, identified himself, and she opened it hesitantly and peered up at him. "I bet he got away, didn't he?" She asked in disgust.

He stepped inside and closed the door behind her. After he looked over to see Nikolai still sleeping, he nodded. "Yes, but he'll be on the cameras, so I'm heading there now."

"That's what I thought," she said. "I didn't want to open the door and run the risk of him coming in on me."

"No, your job is always to look after Nikolai." Mountain walked over and studied the sleeping man. "He does look better, doesn't he?"

"He really does. I'm thinking he'll pull through this just fine."

He looked over at her and smiled. "With his special nurse, I imagine he will."

She flushed bright red and then shrugged.

"It's not wrong to care," Mountain shared.

"But it is wrong to care and to not do anything about it?"

He studied her and then nodded. "I've never heard that, but it's not a bad sentiment to live by." Then he shook his head. "I'll go check the cameras and will be right back." He turned to look at her, before stepping out. "Make sure you lock up." And, with that, he was gone.

She quickly locked the door again, but, within a couple minutes, she heard keys in the door, and it opened, just as she jumped up to take a fighting stance.

Sydney stepped in and stood there, glaring. "What?"

Emily quickly explained, and Sydney's eyebrows shot up. "Oh, Emily, I'm sorry. It briefly crossed my mind that we could have a visitor, but I didn't seriously think anybody would try it. I never would have left you here all alone, if I'd thought it through. I'm sorry."

Emily stared at her and frowned. "This is what I do," she stated, with a smile. "I know everybody sees it differently, but I'm quite capable of protecting him."

"And you did," Sydney acknowledged. "I'm happy for that."

"Mountain told me that he would be back in a little bit. He's gone to see what the cameras caught."

"Good, I'm interested in that myself." She frowned. "How has Nikolai been?"

"Good. A little restless at times but sleeping fairly well."

"That's what I would expect at this stage." The doc checked him over. "Seems he's doing fine."

"Good."

At that, Sydney studied Emily closely and then faced

Nikolai. "You can go back to sleep now, if you want. You'll need to get some rest, especially if you want to keep this up."

Emily frowned and shook her head. "I would rather stay here and see if they found a face to put on whoever was here. I would certainly sleep better if that was resolved."

"You can wait a little bit if you want, but no guarantee that Mountain will be back anytime soon."

"He should be. The cameras aren't all that complex."

"No, but we've had times when the cameras have been shut down or otherwise disabled," Sydney noted, with a wry look in her direction. "So, just because there *should* be pictures doesn't mean there will be. I presume Mountain chased after him?"

"He did, but lost him somewhere." Emily frowned at that, bewildered. "I don't quite understand how and where."

"How long has he been gone?"

"Oh, coming up on an hour I would say."

Sydney nodded. "Which means the intruder's not inside, and, when Mountain checked outside, he couldn't find tracks."

"How the hell does somebody not find tracks out there?" Emily asked, staring at Sydney.

"That's one of the biggest questions we have to solve," she admitted, with a half smile. "But the good news is, we don't have to solve it alone."

When an odd noise came beside them, they both turned immediately to see Nikolai shifting on his bed, trying to sit up. Propping himself on his arms, he looked at them, half asleep.

Sydney walked over and said, "Hey, go back to sleep. You need to rest in order to heal." When he frowned, she laughed at him. "Yes, I'm ordering you back to sleep."

He collapsed on the bed and stared at her. "It wouldn't be so bad if I wasn't alone here."

She rolled her eyes. "I'll say that's the medication and God-only-knows whatever else they have pumping through your system."

His eyes widened, and he groaned. "I think I'm going to be sick."

Sydney was nothing if not fast and somehow came up with a bucket in hand, as if she had some idea of what to expect. He immediately upchucked into the bucket. She smiled back at Emily, then faced Nikolai again. "Good, do that again if you can."

He vomited several more times. When he looked back at her, he asked in confusion, "Why didn't you do that to me earlier?"

"I did," she stated, with a grin. "You probably don't remember, but, as soon as you came in, I had you do that, but I was half expecting more to be coming up as it worked its way through your system. It's like that sometimes," she noted. "Some guys can handle it, and sometimes they stay nauseous for a while."

"In other words, no tea or coffee or cinnamon buns," Emily noted, with a cheeky grin. He glared at her, and she laughed. "You can't be doing too bad if you can give me that dirty look," she stated.

"Did I hear voices earlier?" he asked. "It seemed, I don't know, *wrong* somehow."

"Yeah, *wrong* is a good word for it."

At that, the door opened, and Mountain stepped back in again, but obviously he was not impressed.

"I presume the cameras were out again," Sydney guessed, as she looked at him.

Mountain nodded, looked over at the patient and the bucket beside him, and grimaced. "Isn't that fun?"

"No," Nikolai replied shortly, "it feels like shit."

"Yeah, it sure does, but just wait until it comes out the other end. Then it really will be shit."

Nikolai stared at him for a moment, while he processed the words, then he laughed. "Oh, good, something to look forward to." He looked back over at Mountain. "I would laugh more, but everything hurts like hell. What did she mean about something being *out?*"

Mountain hesitated and then thought it better to keep the patient informed. "You had a visitor while you were out cold."

Nikolai stared, from one to the other. "Who was it?"

"I don't know," Emily replied. "I chose not to open the door."

He stared at her and frowned. "But we could have seen who it was."

She nodded. "My primary objective was keeping you safe. If somebody was trying to break in, there's a good chance they were coming in with a weapon, which would have put you in danger." He stiffened and glared, and she stiffened and glared right back.

"She did exactly what she was supposed to do," Sydney intervened before it turned into an argument. "So don't get angry at her. If you'll get angry at anybody, get angry at me."

"And me," Mountain added, staring at him.

"You didn't let her go after him?"

"Hell no. She contacted me when the intruder tried to get into the door, and unfortunately I lost him. I'm plenty pissed about that."

"How could you lose him though?" Nikolai asked.

"How is that even possible to lose anybody in this compound?"

"That's another thing we have to figure out," Mountain shared. "Either there are hidden depths to this base that we don't know about or someone has another hidey-hole close by."

"I'm surprised you didn't go back out after him," Sydney said, looking at him.

"I checked outside for tracks, and I couldn't find any, which means the intruder must be inside. And, in case you don't know, everybody's been rousted from their beds for that check right now. I'm here to make sure nobody else is in the medical clinic."

She stared at him and then looked around at the others. "It's just us."

"Good," he replied, his voice ever-so-gentle. "Keep it that way." And, with that, he was gone.

NIKOLAI WOKE SEVERAL times in the night, mostly a case of a change in awareness, confusion over where he was, and that inner sense of something wrong. Even as he woke and drifted off to sleep again, several times he saw Emily on the other bed and surmised that she had refused to return to her quarters, choosing instead to stay with him.

He appreciated her concern but didn't want her to think that he was infirm or lacking. Such a strange thing to find himself in the position of needing care. He'd always been one of those tough, strong guys who never needed help. Yet here he was, as least until the drugs were out of his system.

When he woke the next time, Emily was still crashed in

the other hospital bed beside him and Sydney sat at her desk, filling out some paperwork. Sydney looked up, saw him awake, and walked over.

He nodded at Emily. "Did she stay all night?"

"She did, indeed," the doc confirmed. "I suggested she head back several times, but she wasn't interested. She seemed to think that the intruder might come back again."

"I doubt it," Nikolai said, "and, the more I think about it, he may have wanted to talk."

"Which might lend credence to the idea that he was working with your friend, Eric."

"Maybe," he acknowledged, "and, if that's the case, he's likely to be just as well versed in survival out there as anybody else in this place."

"They do have a much better idea of what they're looking for now at least," Sydney added, with a nod.

"Maybe we need to take the dogs out," Nikolai suggested, "because, if a tracker is among them …" Then he frowned. "One of the two dogs that were shot, he's a tracker."

At that, she eyed him intently. "And you know that for sure?"

"Yes," he declared. "I didn't want to bring it up earlier, but I'm wondering if maybe that one was shot on purpose. To put him out of commission, so that everybody here was even more vulnerable."

"And anybody who would shoot a dog …"

"I know. Believe me. I'm right there with you," Nikolai stated. "Imagine what someone like that could do to humans. The world's a shitty place, and sometimes really shitty people are in it."

She smiled and nodded. "And sometimes really good

people are in it, and we can't hold them accountable for all the rest of those shits out there."

He laughed, feeling remarkably good. He pulled back the covers and tried to get up. "I'll make a trip to the washroom."

She got up, helped him to his feet, and double-checked her patient, as he took a few tentative steps. Then she let him stand on his own for a minute, and he looked good to her. "As long as you think you're okay going there alone— otherwise I can give you a hand getting there."

"No, I think I'm fine. You keep an eye on sleeping beauty here." And, with that, he entered the hallway and slowly made his way to the bathroom. As he got there, several other guys stepped out.

"Wow, what the hell happened to you?"

"I spent the night in the medical clinic, for one," he muttered, as he headed inside. He didn't say anything more. When he came back out again, they weren't waiting for him either. But he probably looked pretty green, as if he'd been puking his guts out, which, if he were honest, he had been. Given the choice, he would never want anyone to see him like this. As he headed back to the medical clinic, Magnus waited for him.

"Another minute or two and I would have come to get you."

"If I'd needed another minute or two, I probably would have needed the help," Nikolai admitted, with a smile. "As it is, I think I'll make it."

"I'm glad to hear that."

As they stepped inside, Emily opened her eyes and bolted upright in bed. She looked around, almost panicked, and then she saw Nikolai heading to his bed. "You look much better." She pushed her hair out of her eyes. "Probably better than me at the moment."

"I doubt it, but you look beautiful as you are," he replied, with a smile. "And I'm feeling much better too."

"Good." She flushed at his words. "And it does matter to me by the way, but I definitely need to make a trip to the ladies' room." And, with that, she bounded up and headed outside, full of energy.

Nikolai looked back at Magnus. "That dose of energy is what I need. I'm still feeling on the rough side right now."

"Of course you are," Magnus agreed, "but, according to Sydney, you got some sleep at least."

"I did, and I'm feeling much better than I was. She emptied my stomach, and I did a bunch of dry heaving, just to make me really appreciate the idea of getting some payback for the asshole who drugged me," he muttered. "I never did hear the outcome of the search last night."

"Nothing," Magnus muttered, "the cameras were disabled. Not broken but they were turned around, so somebody knew where they were and shifted them, rather than tearing them out."

"So, in other words, this asshole is probably laughing at us right now," he said, studying Magnus carefully.

Magnus winced. "Yeah, it's kind of like that, isn't it?"

"It sure sounds that way to me," he muttered, "and that sure seems like something Eric would do for sure. But … I can't believe it's Eric in the morgue."

"Agreed. So, the question is, who the hell was he working with … or for?" Magnus asked, looking around thoughtfully.

DAY 4 BREAKFAST

EMILY SAT IN the cafeteria area and ate breakfast. She would bring back something for Nikolai, but his stomach was still too touchy to get food down. Under orders to go and feed herself, she'd come in, picked up some food, and sat in the far corner on her own.

She didn't want to talk to people. She was still rattled about the deadly attack on Nikolai, not to mention the visitor they'd had during the night. It made her even more concerned about everything going on.

Several of the guys she'd seen around had stopped and asked if she was okay. She nodded, while one of them called out, "She hasn't slept well. Have you?"

"I don't think any of us did, after being rousted in the damn night," he replied, as he took a seat across from her.

She nodded. "Right? Not exactly helpful for going back to sleep either."

He snorted at that.

Another buddy joined them, and very quickly her table was full. It was a surprise because it had been a while since anybody had been that friendly. But again, calamity brought people together, and maybe that was a good thing, or maybe she didn't know anything at all. She wanted to hurry and finish, but she didn't want to be rude and break up any conversation that might happen too.

"Any idea if they found anybody?" one of the guys asked her.

She shook her head. "Not that I know of."

"If anybody here would know, it'd be you," he noted cheerfully. She frowned at him, and he shrugged. "You think everybody doesn't know you're one of the favorites?"

Frowning, she shook her head. "I'm certainly not one of the favorites. I'm not even sure any *favorites* are here."

At that, he laughed. "That proves it."

She wasn't sure what to make of it or of the odd grins on their faces. "I'm not sure what you guys are talking about, but, no, I don't know about anything that happened."

They looked at her in a way that was more of a leer.

She winced, not at all sure she liked what they were implying, but was determined to stay out of trouble if she could.

Then one of the men stated, "We're looking at having a party here tonight or maybe tomorrow night. Why don't you join us?"

She hesitated, not sure what kind of party they were talking about. "Hardly seems like a party atmosphere," she murmured.

"Maybe that's why we need to do something," he added. "You can come join us."

She gave him a half smile. "Yeah, I'll be sleeping though. I didn't get any sleep last night, so you can bet I'll be trying to tank up on that commodity tonight."

"Maybe you need somebody to sleep with," he suggested, with a snide tone.

She stiffened slowly and then looked directly at him, with a searching gaze. "I really don't." And, with that, she got up and walked out.

She may have left the table, but his comments stayed with her for the rest of the day, as she headed over to visit with Joe and came back looking in on Nikolai several times. When she returned later that afternoon, Nikolai called her over and took her hand.

"Will you tell me what's going on?"

She looked at him in a surprise, then shrugged. "Nothing to tell, really. Just guys being guys."

He frowned. "Somebody hit on you?"

"More or less," she muttered, "but it wasn't anywhere near that polite."

His eyebrows shot up. "Maybe you should explain that."

"Maybe … I shouldn't," she disagreed cheerfully. "It'll piss you off, and neither of us needs that right now."

"I don't have much of a temper," he declared in a hard voice, "although it's definitely looking as if some payback is in order for what just happened."

"Right, and you're also looking for a target," she noted, with a smile, "and I won't give you one."

"If somebody was treating you shitty," Nikolai said, "you don't have to put up with it. That's the last thing you need around here."

"Not necessary," she replied, "and I'm not sure I would even call it shitty. Some women might take it as a compliment."

"But not you, right?"

"No, not me, not this time anyway," she explained, "and not the way it was done. It was more insulting than anything."

He stared at her. "You're really not helping your case."

"You mean, I'm not helping *their* case, but you, on the other hand, don't know what happened. So you won't say anything," she said cheerfully.

When Magnus came back a little later, he spoke to both of them. "A couple meetings will be happening. One is in the cafeteria right now." He looked at her pointedly. "It's important for you to attend."

She nodded, getting up and saying, "I'll go now then, and, after that, I'll come find you. What kind of a meeting is it?"

"You won't be participating," he explained. "I will, and a couple of the leaders will be there to see it through," he added. "And hopefully we'll get to the bottom of this."

"If there's a bottom to get to, I'm sure you will," she noted, as she quickly walked out the door.

In the mess area, she quickly grabbed a coffee and took a seat, where she could listen to what was coming down the pipeline. As the same group of men came in, the first two immediately leered at her. She wasn't sure where or how they had even gotten that idea about her or where the sudden interest was coming from, but she didn't like it. She would have to do something to stop it immediately, which was a little hard, considering that the colonel then stepped into the room and immediately gave them the rundown on the intruder.

"As you all well know, we did a full-on search of the compound last night, and we didn't find what we were looking for."

"Maybe that means nobody is here," one of the men muttered, under his breath.

"We need you to all be alert. We've had another person attacked, drugged, and almost killed," he relayed. Shocked murmurs came around her, but, as she already knew this, she didn't say anything or look in anyone's direction, particularly those leering men. Something was very off-putting about the two of them. There had been four in the original group, but the irritation was being led by these guys.

"Quiet!" the CO roared.

At that, the murmuring died instantly.

"I want to draw your attention to ensuring that all the equipment is double- and triple-checked, safety protocols are followed to extreme levels, and you are watching out for everybody, including those who you think are not a problem. Absolutely no way at the moment to know who's doing this, but I can tell you right now. We will find out, and it won't take us long."

And, with that, he turned and walked out.

Almost immediately came catcalls and muted boos behind the CO.

She was astonished because, although people often didn't like the brass, obvious displays of this kind were considered mutinous and were never ever allowed. She listened to some of it, and, not liking what she heard, she got up, refilled her coffee. As she went to step out of the room, one of the same leering men stepped in front of her.

"You need to rethink our invitation."

"Ah, no. I don't need to rethink it at all."

"You think we didn't know that you weren't in your room last night?" he asked, with a sneer. "You think you're too good for us?"

She looked at him with a flash of anger. "Seriously, that's what this is about? You realized I wasn't sleeping in my room, so, therefore, I must have been whoring myself off for somebody else, and you were left high and dry without it?" she snapped in a mocking tone.

He flushed and glared.

"For your information, I was on guard duty," Emily stated. "Something that maybe you should think about doing. But, oh wait, you're not cleared for it, are you?" Not responding any further, she turned and walked out of the dining room. She hadn't gone very far when Chef Elijah came racing behind her. She turned and looked at him. "Hey."

He grumbled at the men behind him, who were still staring back at her, half in shock, half in dismay, but very disgruntled, as Chef muttered, "If they're giving you any trouble, you let me know."

She shrugged and then in a loud and clear voice, she replied, "The day I let assholes like that cause me worry is the day I need to leave the military."

Chef grinned. "Still, that was uncalled for on their part, and that is definitely sexual harassment, if you want to put in a complaint."

She rolled her eyes. "That'll make me very unpopular around this place in a hurry," she muttered.

"Might keep you alive and sane too," Chef added.

"No, it's all right. Did you have a reason for calling me down?"

He laughed and nodded. "Yeah, if you can, the doc wants you to take some food down to our patient," he said, with a smile.

"Oh, good, he must be feeling better," she replied quickly. "Sorry, those guys kind of threw me off."

"Come on over and get it," he said, as they walked back into the kitchen area. The other men were still standing around, watching. She tossed them both a look, and one immediately turned away his gaze.

"Yeah, you better look away, asshole," she muttered to

herself. The last thing she needed was that kind of harassment, but unfortunately it was incredibly common. Most of the time she could handle it just fine, but up here, right now? Everybody was on the edge of more ugliness, and who knew where it would end up.

By the time Chef Elijah had a breakfast tray made up for Nikolai, the leering guys had left. She headed out the hallway, carrying the tray past several people who didn't say anything to her, which was good as far as she was concerned. By the time she made it to the medical clinic, she stopped and tapped at the door with her foot, to let them know she was there.

Sydney opened the door immediately and smiled when she saw the food. "Glad to know Chef caught you."

"I could've gone back again too," Emily suggested, with a smile.

She shrugged. "But since you were already there, it made sense."

Emily carried the tray inside and set it down for Nikolai.

"A tray? God help me, I told her that I could eat on my own. I'm not an invalid."

"I understood your stomach was feeling rough enough still that you weren't ready to eat just anything yet," Emily pointed out, with a smile. "So, I was quite happy to hear that I should bring this," she teased. "And, hey, if nothing else, I can watch you eat it and then upchuck it all over again."

He glared at her and then laughed. "Yeah, you must feel better to be on *that* side of it," he admitted, "because it's not anything I've ever particularly enjoyed."

"Didn't you go through that stage when you were younger where you drank so much you puked constantly?"

"Yeah, *once*," he admitted, "but I learned very quickly

not to overdo it after that."

"I think it's a constant for some people," she noted, "but I'm glad you figured out what caused it."

He grinned and looked at what she brought him. "What? No cinnamon buns," he asked, with a bit of a whining tone.

"Nope. I brought you what Chef Elijah determined that you could have. And believe me. I'm not going against him."

He grinned. "He's a big man, and he can be kind of scary when he wants."

"He also controls the grub," she added, with a bright smile. "Nobody smart will cross him."

"Right, which is why the kitchen fires are kind of odd, right?"

"Or not. Maybe they are just the facts of life when working on a military base, short-staffed, and always racing to get things done." Emily shrugged. "I sure don't blame anybody in that kitchen if they have a little bit of a mishap happening now and then."

"I know, and I get it. I hear you, and I'm not trying to blame anybody over there."

"Good, because he's looking out for you."

"I'm glad to hear that." Nikolai picked up a fork and a bit of scrambled egg and took a bite cautiously, as if afraid it wouldn't stay down. But he slowly managed to eat about half of his breakfast and then looked at the rest and grumbled. "I can't. Any more and I will …"

"Got it," Emily said. "I was surprised he put so much on your plate, then thought maybe you would need it later."

"But cold eggs never appeal." Nikolai looked down at it. "Do you want any?"

"I had some breakfast earlier, but I wasn't terribly hungry."

"Then have some of this," he offered immediately, "Nobody's here to watch. Especially not them."

She looked at him. "How did you know those guys were there?"

"Did they hassle you again?" he asked, his gaze hard.

"They apparently saw that my room was empty last night, when the check was going on."

"And?" he asked in confusion. "What's that got to do with anything?"

"I think they were under an inaccurate impression. In fact, I asked them myself if they were upset because they thought I was whoring around the compound, and they were missing out on getting some." He flushed dark red in fury, and she held up her hand. "You don't get to be upset about this," she stated, shutting him down. "I told them flat-out that I was on guard duty and that they needed to leave me the hell alone."

She hadn't actually said that last part out loud, but she was pretty sure they'd gotten the message.

He shook his head. "You shouldn't have to handle that."

"No, I shouldn't, and Elijah said something to me about it too." Emily smiled. "He told me that I should report them for sexual harassment."

Beside her, Sydney nodded. "He's right. You should."

"But you know what that would be like in this place right now," she stated, looking back at her. "It's already tough enough to go out there and to deal with people who are all worried and half panicked over everything," she explained, shaking her head. "That's really not something I want to bring up right now."

"And yet when would you bring it up?" he asked her.

"Because, after you leave here, you won't."

"No, I won't," she admitted, facing him. "Why would I? It's always harder on those making the complaint, and I sure as hell wouldn't want to be interrogated over it. Plus, I don't have any proof."

"Nobody else was around there?"

"Sure, his buddies, as if that'll make a difference."

Looking over at her intently, Sydney frowned. "If it gets worse, if they come back after you or anything escalates, you need to let other people know."

Nonplussed by their concern, Emily nodded. "Fine, I'll let you know if it gets any worse, but I suspect that they'll back away now."

"Maybe not," Nikolai said. "Sometimes guys like that will just go underground and jump you at some point in time when you least expect it."

She winced at that. "Thank you for that image. As if we don't have enough problems in this damn place already."

"But problems like that are exactly what makes these guys go off the rails. They're scared. They're looking for answers. They want something to punch, and, if they can't do it physically, they'll do it sexually."

She shook her head. "These men should be disciplined enough to go through a training session without needing that, right?"

"Maybe," Nikolai muttered, "and, in an ideal world, that might be a good answer. I'm not sure that we have an ideal world here. Plus, if they really did have that opinion of you, that sucks. Where the hell are they getting that impression? And why would they think they could act on it?"

"It's the acting on it that bothers me," Sydney noted. "You do have to worry in a place like this." She turned to

Nikolai. "As women, we are always wary. But also, in a case like this, I can see her point. Emily has been here for a long time. She doesn't feel there's a problem, and, until today, there wasn't a problem, correct?"

Emily nodded. "Correct, and maybe the nighttime checkups have people rattled again. I don't know what it is, but definitely an anger, a frustration, an uneasiness is there. The thought that somebody is walking around this base, who isn't a registered attendee, is troublesome. And the whole thing with Eric has everybody upset ... on multiple levels." Emily took a moment to add, "I think everybody's kind of spooked, and this is maybe their way of handling that."

"If that's their way of handling it, they've got a surprise coming," Nikolai snapped.

She looked at him. "You are stuck in bed, and you need to stay here, until Sydney lets you off the hook."

He gave her a ghost of a smile. "If you think for one second that I'm not capable of handling those assholes over something like that, even in this condition," he told her, his voice taking on a silky tone, "you don't know me very well."

She glared at him. "I *don't* know you very well. I'm hoping to get to know you better, but you need to behave yourself long enough to get yourself out of here," she declared, "because I firmly believe that Sydney can kick your butt across this room, sick or not, to ensure that you follow her orders." He was taken aback by this turn of events, until she looked him square in the eyes and snarled. "Do you hear me?" When he stayed quiet, she growled at him again. "Do you?"

He looked at her in surprise and then a slow, dawning grin crossed over his face.

"What?"

"I really like that you can stand up to me," he said. "A lot of women act as if they're terrified."

"You're a big man. I'll give you that. I'm sure, in some ways, those other women are scared of that. I, however, am not. So don't ever think that will make me back off."

Sydney, who was now grinning broadly, added, "Didn't I hear something about you having black belts in multiple disciplines?"

Emily snorted. "Not sure where you heard that, but, yes, that's correct, and, yes, I'm perfectly capable of kicking his ass into tomorrow, but I'm sure he would put up a good fight for it."

"No, I wouldn't," Nikolai argued. "You're trying to help me here. So, while I might get pissed off, confused, fed up, and maybe a little turned on, I would never ever hurt you."

"I know that," Emily declared, "and that gives me the advantage."

"Oh my God, both of you, play nice for a change," Sydney replied. "I'll go get some fresh coffee and see if I can roust up some breakfast for myself. Do you guys think you can stay out of trouble for a few minutes?" As they nodded, she smiled and turned to leave. "I'll be back in five, so don't get up to anything that takes longer than that." And, with that, she was gone, leaving them both staring at the open door.

Emily asked, "Did she really say that?"

He grinned. "She absolutely did." He chuckled. "I really like her."

"I do too," Emily agreed, with a smile, "but I really didn't expect that."

"I'm sure she would say that we're bickering like an old married couple," he shared, with a smile. "Honestly, the way we're acting, she's probably not far off."

Emily groaned. "I hope that's not how we're acting because that would be pretty depressing."

"Why is that?" he asked.

"I would prefer to think that we have a little more going for us than squabbling."

He winced. "Pretty sure we do," he agreed. "I have to get out of this damn hospital bed first to prove it."

"No, you absolutely do not have to prove it," she argued, with a smile. "I already know lots about you. I've seen you out there in training. I know that you've been pretty upset all this time at the disappearance and the loss of your friend, and now you're dealing with the confusion and betrayal, as we've uncovered these new revelations. And still we don't know quite what Eric was up to," she admitted, with a headshake. "You can learn an awful lot about people when you watch them."

He studied her and slowly nodded. "Agreed. I've always been one of those guys who was in the background, watching everybody else, wondering what made them tick, trying to figure it out," he shared, smirking. "Sometimes it works. Sometimes it doesn't. Sometimes it's good, and sometimes you sit there in shock and stare at them, trying to understand what made them do what they did."

She laughed. "Yeah, I've seen a few things like that myself. People themselves are fascinating, but the shit they can do? Yeah, that's not so much fun."

"Agreed. ... What will you do now?"

"I didn't get a ton of sleep last night, but I did get some, so I'm not sure what I'll do," she said. "I haven't checked in with anybody to even see what's on my schedule today."

"Maybe go check the duty roster and see where you're

at." When she hesitated, he added, "Go on. It's daytime. I'm fine."

She shook her head. "I'll wait until Sydney comes back." He glared at her, and she glared right back. Thankfully Sydney came in a few minutes later and saw the two of them locked in a staring contest.

"Maybe if you two got a room or something, it would help," the doc suggested.

"If we got a room," Nikolai stated, "it would help a lot, but I don't think anybody will let us have a room, not unless you release me."

"I was wondering how you were doing, and I would really like to see if your breakfast stays down first," Sydney replied, smiling.

"Emily won't leave because she's afraid something'll go wrong."

"Hey, I told you that I was waiting for Sydney to get back," she repeated, glaring at him again.

"I'm fine," he said in protest.

"Yeah, I know. You're cranky, so you are definitely getting better," she declared, with an eye roll, as she looked over at Sydney. "Do you need me at all? Can you use me? Is there anything I can do for you?"

Sydney shook her head. "Nope. Go. Go off and do something else. I'm sure I'll have this guy released pretty quickly." She turned to look at Nikolai and added, "Assuming he behaves."

"If you say so," Emily quipped, "but I really wouldn't be too quick about it. He obviously needs to be in here for a while longer." He frowned at that, and she smiled at him sweetly. "As you can tell, he's definitely cranky."

"Oh, he's cranky all right," Sydney agreed, laughing,

"but you're looking a little stressed yourself."

"Yeah, because he's trying to go back out there and fight off all the bad guys in the world," she muttered, as she walked toward the door. "That isn't happening, particularly not until he's back on his feet and done tossing his cookies." And, with that retort, she headed out to start her day, whatever that might be.

⊕

AFTER EMILY WAS gone, Nikolai sank back into his hospital bed and looked over at Sydney. "Do you get many sexual assault victims?"

"Not if I can help it," she declared, "and never twice, but it's very hard to get women to report them."

"Jesus, so it really is a problem."

"Absolutely. Don't kid yourself because it doesn't matter which faction of service you're talking about. It's a problem. Wherever a large congregation of men and a much smaller group of women gather, you'll get these problems."

"Do you think these guys will go after her?"

She looked at him steadily for a moment. "I can only say that, the longer we're here, the more likely it is to happen."

"That's bullshit," he snapped, staring at her in shock. "The women are as vulnerable here as they are anywhere, more so if anything, so the men should be trying to protect them."

"And yet, in this case, the opposite is often the case. They'll gang up together, and it'll be a free-for-all."

He winced. "God, I don't want to hear that."

She shrugged. "You might not want to hear it, and I can tell you that the brass really doesn't want to hear it either.

But a lot of the women here think they're strong and capable enough because they go through the same training as the men do. But it doesn't take much for one or two or three guys to decide that some woman should be a little friendlier. And, when it's more than one man, most of the women are completely overwhelmed and can't protect themselves," she explained in a flat tone.

Sydney continued. "It's one thing to have skills on a level playing field, but it's another thing to have skills where you have a hidden advantage, like the advantage of surprise," she pointed out. "In that case, where it's sexual assault, generally the women are not on a level playing field. Sometimes because of sheer strength and size alone, or worse, sometimes they are literally outnumbered." Sydney sighed. "Some are drugged. You were taken out that way."

"So, am I free to go?" Nikolai asked.

"It depends. What's your plan?"

He winced. "I would like to say, *Keeping an eye on her*, but she would probably have my head for that."

"She might, but then again she might need it too."

"What do you mean?" he asked, fear creeping up on him.

"I don't know what these guys are up to or even who it is she's having trouble with. However, I do know that the atmosphere out there is definitely ugly and getting uglier," the doc replied, with a shake of her head. "I'm about to have a meeting with the colonel and Mountain about it because it'll get worse before it gets better, and I would like to head that off, *before* we get there."

He stared at her for a long moment. "In that case, clear me to go, and I'll keep an eye on her. I've already been told to keep an eye on her, and I can't do that here."

Sydney hesitated, and then she shrugged. "As far as I'm concerned, medically you're sound. Just take it easy and see how that food stays in your system."

"It didn't come back up, and it's been over an hour."

"That's not necessarily long enough to say that you're good to go," she pointed out, "but I'll take it for now. If you have any problems, get your ass back in here, and I mean that." She added, "Look. I'm heading into a meeting with Mountain, so don't mess that up because it's important too."

"I get that."

Then Mountain stepped in and asked them both, "Did I hear my name mentioned?"

"Yes," Sydney confirmed. "I believe we're going to a meeting."

"We are," he said. "I wanted to see if you were ready."

Nikolai interrupted, "Before you go, I need to tell you about something." And he quickly explained the harassment that Emily had described.

Mountain's eyebrows shot up. "Damn it," he spat in a furious tone. "Is that what you want to meet about?" he asked, looking over at Sydney.

"Not specific to Emily, but yes. This is a potential side effect of our situation, yeah," she stated, with a nod. "It could go in that direction, but I think we'll also see more fights, more arguments, and more shit happening, one way or another."

"What do you think we should do about it?"

Sydney smiled. "Keep the women on a strict buddy system. Plus work everyone hard. Get them out there doing something, anything, so they come back too exhausted to even think about anything else."

He frowned but nodded. "Let's go talk to the boss."

"What about me?" Nikolai asked, knowing that it didn't matter what they would tell him, he would do what he thought needed to be done.

Mountain looked at him, waved his hand to cut off whatever argument Nikolai would make. "Say no more." Mountain was grinning now. "From the looks of it, no matter what I say, you'll do what you think is right. So go keep an eye on her—if she'll let you. I think she's over with the dogs."

"Oh, good," Nikolai said. "I wanted to talk to Joe again anyway."

"Anything I should know about?" Mountain asked, gazing at him.

He shrugged and shook his head. "No, but, of all the places for our intruder to go and hide, that would be one of the easiest."

"Explain."

"An awful lot of feed is stacked in the back corners," Nikolai pointed out, "and an awful lot of dark places are in the dog barn, where somebody could hide. If that didn't get checked last night into this morning, I'm sure my visitor's long gone by now. Still, I wanted to ask Joe if somebody was coming and going from that area of the compound."

Mountain stared at him for a long moment. "You do a full check on that, and I want a report." He glanced at his watch and motioned Sydney out, then called back to Nikolai, "Meet me in an hour. As soon as this meeting is over, I want to know what you found."

And, with that, the two of them were gone.

DAY 4 AFTERNOON

EMILY WAS DISTRACTED, finding it hard to keep focused on her work, especially when wondering how Nikolai was doing. Yet the fact that her work assignment today was physically taxing helped a lot. She was working on the skis for the sleds, which always needed to be waxed. The winter weather here in the Great White North was known for snow coverage. However, when it became an icy crust, it ate through the wax coating on the skis pretty fast.

She warmed up the wax, using the hot irons that stayed on the wood stove, in order to apply the wax. All kinds of modern methods were available, but Joe preferred the old traditions, and she was okay with it. She found it relaxing actually, almost numbing. She could do what she needed to do, but, in the end, physically exhausting enough that it kept her thoughts of worry about Nikolai at bay.

Emily kept her head down and continued to work hard. When Joe called out to her a little later, she looked up to find Nikolai standing there, grinning at her, his big hands cuddling a blissful Bertie. Emily immediately stepped back from the skis and glared at him. "What are you doing up?" She was beyond mad.

He rolled his eyes at her. "How did I know that would be your first response?" he muttered, with a twinkle in his blue eyes.

She shook her head. "You should be lying down."

He laughed. "Like hell." He gave her a teasing smile. "I've been there, done that, and I'm not going back again. Sydney also cleared me, by the way. I can go to bed at my own discretion"—he waggled his eyebrows—"as long as I'm not alone."

She flushed and cast a quick glance over to Joe, who was grinning broadly, happy in his own world. She sighed. "You shouldn't say things like that," she muttered.

"Maybe not." He gave a careless shrug. "I don't particularly care at the moment."

"What are you doing out here?"

"I was here earlier, checking something out," he shared, his face turning serious. "And now I'm back again, looking at something else. You keep doing what you're doing, and I'll do my own thing over here."

"Now that you've interrupted me, I can't ignore you."

"Oh, good. I'm glad to hear that I'm not easily ignorable."

"Sometimes you're very ignorable," she pointed out in a sarcastic drawl. "But right now? Whatever you're doing is making me curious, so I want to know what it is."

"In that case, you'll have to wait," he said, holding up a finger. "I'm back again to look more closely out here."

"What are you getting at?"

"I wondered if someone could have been hiding out here."

"I hadn't even considered that," she noted, taken aback. "I guess it would be pretty warm though, wouldn't it?"

"The thing is, you would only need to hide here temporarily. And, if you think about it, if you made friends with the dogs, they wouldn't alert anybody, and, if you curled up in the back here and hid until the search had passed, there wouldn't be any tracks outside. There would be nothing. Even if you cut out early from here, your tracks would be absorbed, obliterated, as this whole area is packed with dog tracks."

She slowly nodded. "Is that what you think happened last night, earlier this morning?" she asked in a hoarse whisper.

"I don't know what to think, so that's why I'm here, doing another check."

"It's a pretty small space, compared to the base."

"It is. It definitely is," Nikolai agreed, "but some of the potential hidey-holes we find when we're in these small places are pretty freaking amazing. Just let me be for a bit."

She shrugged and went back to her work, watching out of the corner of her eye as he went corner to corner, checking everything out. When he returned, he had a frown on his face. "So, I presume you didn't find anything."

"No, I didn't, and yet I can't leave it alone."

"Okay, what is it you're expecting to find? Maybe we can start with that."

He shrugged. "A place to hide, as I mentioned. A simple place to hide. Temporarily or as long as any search is happening."

She got up and looked around. She pointed to the huge bin for gear storage. "So, I guess that's technically one place."

He walked over, lifted the lid, and nodded. "It's definitely big enough to hide somebody."

"But they wouldn't have access to an escape very quickly though," she pointed out. "So, as a hiding place, it would do temporarily but not for long."

Nikolai agreed. "We're up against that scenario anyway.

All they need is a place to get away from the main complex, and they could be here in a heartbeat."

She looked around and slowly nodded. "And yet what's to stop Joe from finding them?"

"It's not that anything would stop Joe from finding them—but Joe." Nikolai gave her a wry smile and whispered, "Did you know that he enjoys a couple drinks in the evening?"

She stared at him in surprise and then slowly added, "So, you're thinking somebody would have taken advantage of that and come and gone. If the dogs know who our intruder is, maybe he brings treats for the dogs, and they might yip and yelp, getting excited to see him. However, if they were well-trained, which of course these are, the stranger may get in and out without any trouble."

"Exactly," Nikolai muttered, with a look of mixed emotions.

"Is it possible?"

"Yes."

"Is it plausible?"

"I don't know," he said. "That would be the issue."

"Speaking of issues, I think you should be back on the base, lying down," she noted crossly.

He grinned. "Thanks for worrying about me, but don't you want answers?"

"Damn right I want answers," she snapped, raising both hands. "Not having answers is freaking irritating. Not being able to tear things apart to get them is also irritating."

"More to the point," Nikolai added, as he looked around, "we can have this conversation later. Now, is there any other place he could have hidden? A place where he could have come and gone in a way that his presence would have gone undetected?"

She looked around with him, though he'd already done a search of the area. "Those big supply boxes were plausible, but not necessarily very feasible, not with Joe around."

Nikolai eyed her, as he considered that. "We know Joe," he replied in a low voice. "He does have a drink or two in the evenings. He also goes to bed early, and it's quite possible he wouldn't have noticed anything. Which means nothing much would have stopped anyone from coming and going."

She winced at that. "That's still a little bit hard to believe. What about the dogs?" And then she grabbed his arm and pointed in the direction of the dog doors. He stared at them and nodded slowly. "Particularly if Joe wouldn't have heard much," she added in a low voice.

"And the dogs?" he asked.

"Someone could take a little bit of time, get to know them, bring them treats. That's what we're all doing here," she admitted.

Nikolai nodded. "In a way we've all been assigned a dog, and we've all been given time to work with them."

"So, the intruder has already gotten that far with the dogs," she noted. "All he had to do was continue on with the same training."

"So, you're assuming," Nikolai pointed out, "that he was part of our base."

"Eric was, so his partner would smell like him, act like him, talk like him. Plus, if Eric's partner was our intruder, he was in and out and all about with Eric. Therefore, I don't think it would've taken much for Eric's partner to find his way into being comfortable with the dogs. Particularly if he's had time to get to know them. What if he was here last night? Even among the stray people who come and go?"

"Meaning?" Nikolai asked.

She faced him. "Meaning, the pilot, the guy who does the delivery. ... A couple times he's had to stay overnight because the weather was so shitty, and he couldn't take off for another day or two."

Nikolai shrugged. "He's been cleared though."

"Sure, but we don't know that he didn't come in with somebody else. We don't know for sure that he didn't get paid to smuggle somebody in. For all we know, some of this was part of the secret training Eric set up," she suggested. "Maybe it went a little too far, or maybe somebody used that training session to take on an extra mission of their own."

Nikolai held up his finger. "Let's sort out one thing first." He looked over at Joe, who was grumbling at a clipboard in his hand, as he stared at his supplies. With a pencil behind one ear and chewing on the end of a second, he muttered his way through the inventory of some of his stock. Now moving, Nikolai slipped out the dog door.

She watched and realized that at no point in time did Joe realize somebody was using the door because the dogs came and went through those doors all the time. Joe also didn't notice that Nikolai was or wasn't here. When Nikolai returned the same way a little bit later, and stood up, a couple of the dogs jumped on him, anxious to be part of this new game, and he immediately calmed them with a hand signal. He looked over at her with an eyebrow raised, and she slowly shook her head to signify that Joe hadn't even noticed.

He walked back over quietly and held a finger against his lips. "I'll disappear, and then I'll come back that way, with no warning. Let's see how feasible this is."

She nodded and went back to her work, but she kept

looking around, watching to see if Nikolai was here.

Finally, even Joe noticed her worry, as he asked, "What's wrong? Why are you so edgy?"

She groaned. "I don't know. It's one of those days, I guess."

"Well, hurry up and finish and get lost then," he replied, with his usual grumpy tone. "That edginess of yours is making me edgy," he grumbled.

She laughed. "Okay already. I'm almost done here. I'll finish this off and then head back. Besides, I'll need food soon."

"That's what happens when you get too cold just once," Joe explained. "It's like your body, the furnace in your system, constantly needs reinforcement after that. You have to pay attention and don't ever run short again."

"How is that even possible around here?" she asked, with a groan. "Avalon and Chrissy and Chef work hard to feed us pretty well."

"Probably too well." Joe smiled, as he patted his stomach. "We're definitely getting spoiled on this trip, and I understand why—in terms of keeping everybody's spirits up," he noted, "but it'll show up on my waistline."

"Oh, come on. You get tons of exercise."

"According to my wife, my pants are getting a little on the tighter side."

She burst out laughing. "Tell your wife to come here for one of these training sessions and see how well she handles it."

He gave her a fat grin. "Nope, these are my sessions. I want to come alone, and it also gives me a break. Sometimes I want to tune her out. When you've been with somebody for so long that you know what they'll say before they open their mouth, you kind of fall into the habit of not really listening anymore."

"You wouldn't." Emily gasped.

"It's probably not the best thing, but life falls into a bit of a rut when you're together for so long," he shared. "These visits, these missions? They're good for me. They keep me sharp."

She nodded, not sure what to say about that because obviously whatever sharpness he was talking about wasn't something he had displayed so far. "I'm done here, so why don't I head over. Do you want a coffee or something?"

He looked at her and smiled. "Sure, if you feel like delivering it. I used to go over and get things, but, with the weather and the hassle of getting all geared up to go the distance, half the time I can't be bothered. And then, if it's really ugly, I won't even do that much. So, if you're up for it, I won't say no."

"Sure," she said, with a smile. As she exited, she cast one more glance around, saw absolutely nothing amiss and no sign of Nikolai.

She headed into the kitchen area of the base. As soon as she got inside, Mountain looked at her sharply. "Where's Nikolai?"

"Testing out a theory," she replied, "and honestly it's a pretty decent theory too. It won't make one member of this team look very good, and that is something I feel really bad about."

His eyebrows shot up, and he groaned. "You want to explain that?"

She hesitated. "That should be a Nikolai thing." Mountain grumbled at her, and she nodded. "I don't know where he's at right now, but I know he wanted to do a test run to see if his theory was feasible."

"Maybe you should tell me a little bit more about that theory," Mountain said in exasperation.

She shrugged. "Or you could wait a few minutes, and we'll see if it works."

He poured a coffee and turned, almost tapping his feet impatiently. When her phone buzzed, she found a message from Nikolai.

I'm hidden. Can you find me?
In the same location?
Yes.

Then Joe walked in. She promptly slid her phone in a back pocket, as he grinned at her openly. "I decided to come over and get some food anyway, so skip the coffee delivery."

"Okay. I think I must have left my phone over there."

"You better go get it," Joe replied. "You don't want to leave it in those temperatures for too long."

"Even inside your place?"

"Hey, it doesn't take long to cool down electronics."

She nodded and, with Mountain looking puzzled, she motioned at him to follow.

"What are we doing?" Mountain asked, as he geared up, and they headed over to the dog barn.

"Yeah, we're about to go see if we can find Nikolai."

"Where?" he asked.

"With the dogs." As they approached, she explained how Nikolai had gone in and out of the dog run through the dog doors, all without Joe noticing.

Mountain stopped and stared, then nodded once. "And that would make sense."

As they stepped inside, she looked around, frowning. She whispered to Mountain, "Earlier today we thought of multiple places in the barn that could hold a man, where someone could get in or out on their own, and wondered if anybody would notice," she explained. "We assumed that, with a little time to work with the dogs, they wouldn't be a problem, and, if the intruder could find a time when Joe was either tired, not paying attention, sleeping, or whatnot, it might be quite feasible in terms of hiding from him too."

Mountain stared around the dog barn, looking at the stacks of supplies and dogs in multiple corners, and he nodded excitedly. "Okay, at first glance, it doesn't appear anything's here," he muttered, his gaze narrowing, as he walked over to the big storage trunk and quickly opened it.

She winced, thinking that Mountain would find Nikolai right off the bat. But, as soon as the trunk was opened, it was empty. "That's where I thought he would be," she said.

Mountain turned around, found another storage bin, and opened it. Then found a third one, underneath a bunch of tack. He turned to her, frowning. "There isn't any other place in here."

She studied the area, then looked over where Joe's bed was. Walking over, she bent down to look underneath it, but gear was so close by, it was hard to see. Letting her eyes adjust, it didn't take long to see Nikolai under there, grinning at her.

He slowly came out and Mountain glared at them. "Damn it."

"I know." Nikolai grinned broadly. "If you hadn't known I was supposed to be here, would you have found me?"

Mountain shook his head. "No," he snapped, harsher than he intended. "And did you get in through the dog door while Joe was here?" he asked, with a questioning look at him.

Nikolai nodded. "Yes, that's exactly how I got in and out—a couple times actually. The dogs are quite happy to play the game. So, with anybody who's done it a time or two, the dogs would be completely okay. But, even in a pinch, this is how they're getting in and out and away from here. Plus, no tracks were anywhere close by, and the dog doors lead out to the dog runs which are covered—wait for it—in dog tracks. So it probably isn't all that hard to camouflage your own footprints."

"Sure, it is," Mountain countered. "Yet now we know more about what to look for."

At that, she made a strangled noise in the back of her throat. "If you look closely at all the prints out there, remember how Joe has been creating boots for a lot of the dogs to protect them from the ice?" Mountain nodded, and she walked over and pointed out several examples. "All these will make different-looking tracks. So even having these out there will do a ton to camouflage actual footprints."

Wanting to try it, Mountain went through the dog door himself. It was a tight fit, but then Mountain was huge. When he got out to the other side, she followed, and so did Nikolai. There, the big man walked the pen, carefully looking at the tracks, and, when they got to the far end, he started to swear. "He's gone over the fence at this corner." He pointed to the underbrush there.

"So, that's how he's been getting in and out." Nikolai shook his head.

"Seems like it." Mountain frowned.

"Now the question is whether just Eric was doing this or if this is also where we got our intruder from?" Nikolai asked.

"I'll guess it's both," Emily replied with finality. "Once they found a pathway in and out that they could keep using without being detected, that became a no-brainer."

Mountain nodded. "I'm heading out on these tracks." He looked over at Nikolai, who was already glaring at him.

"I'm coming too," he snapped.

"Yeah, you're coming, as long as you're not hurt," Mountain stated, with a word of warning about his latest injury. They both turned and looked at her, and she nodded.

"I'm coming too."

At that, they both shook their heads vehemently. "No."

She glared at them. "I'm not some hothouse flower that needs to be protected," she snapped. "I've been a part of this, and I want to see it through."

"You are a part of this," Mountain replied, "but I want you to stay here in case this asshole decides to come back in again. With Joe gone and quite likely gone for an hour, what's to stop our intruder from either coming in, crawling out from another hidey-hole"—he frowned at that thought, as he looked back at the barn—"or planning to return for something later?"

"But …"

"No buts, I need you here. We'll follow the tracks, but that doesn't mean he isn't already hidden somewhere close by. It may seem foolish to think that he is, but I'm not comfortable with the idea that he's *not* around," Mountain pointed out. "I'll put a couple other people on alert as well," he noted, as he pulled out his phone. "And we'll ensure our intruder doesn't end up behind us."

"I can help with that," Emily said.

"Nikolai is enough for that, and I will track." He looked over at him. "You any good at tracking?"

Nikolai immediately nodded. "Damn right, I am. Particularly in this case."

"As in?"

"As in tracking men," Nikolai stated, "particularly assholes."

※

NIKOLAI, ENERGIZED BY this turn of events, pushed ahead, strong, with Mountain at his side. They followed the tracks for what seemed to be a good hour. When they made a big circle and started to confuse the footprints as they backtracked on each other, Nikolai paused and studied them carefully.

"What do you see?" Mountain asked, as he looked at the tracks himself and then around the area.

"I see an attempted deception," Nikolai shared, "with too many tracks and no purpose for them. I suggest we make a much bigger circle and see if we can find out where the main tracks lead."

"Given the attempt to hide the tracks, it can't be too far away," Mountain declared, excitedly rubbing his hands. "Keep looking. You'll see it." When Nikolai frowned at him, Mountain nodded. "Yes, I can see it."

"You holding out on me?"

"No, and don't feel bad. I've been doing this for a hell of a long time," Mountain declared, "and right now I'm seriously motivated."

"You and me both." Nikolai turned his attention to study the tracks. "Okay, this track heads off, and it's definitely going somewhere."

"Why is that?" Mountain asked, as they studied the

track.

"It's deeper, heavier, with stronger slides. He's trying to move out quickly."

"Agreed. So, why?"

"I think he's moved his campsite. I think whatever we'll find here has already been moved elsewhere."

"Let's see if we can find what we're looking for, then, and if we can track him to the next place," Mountain said, "because I'm not going back until I find this asshole."

Not surprised at his attitude, and in full agreement, they searched the tracks carefully, looking for a break and for that slight depression in the snow that would tell them where Eric's partner's base had been.

Then Nikolai saw it. "There." He pointed a good twenty meters ahead. Moving forward on his skis, as soon as he came to a stop, Mountain at his side, Nikolai poked the ground in front of him. "Look ahead another ten feet or so."

"I see it," Mountain confirmed, as he unbuckled his skis and carefully moved forward, not sure whether this was a trap or something they needed to be wary of. He used his ski pole to prod the ground, and suddenly the hidden hideaway opened up, and, as suspected, was empty. They took the cover off completely, disappointment eating away at them. Mountain nodded. "We've got him on the run, so that's good."

Nikolai frowned at him. "How is that good?"

"We got close. A few hours earlier and we might have caught him. The fact that we've even found this now, that we know his pattern and how he's coming and going onto the base, it's all good." Shooting him a look, he added, "Good job on that, by the way. We're not far away from catching this asshole."

"Maybe not, but it still feels too damn far away to cheer just yet."

"Oh, I hear you, and I think you're probably right, but we're not so far away that he'll evade us much longer," Mountain stated, as he studied the area. "Finding this now is massive. … Let's take a good look at this and figure out where he's gone from here."

"You check his campsite," Nikolai said, taking a sharp intake of air. "I'll do a wider circle around and see if I can find where he finally takes off."

And with that, going out another mile, but keeping the new location in sight, Nikolai circled around, looking for more tracks. Visibility was terrible, and the wind had picked up, and the snow was flying, but, with a careful and steady gaze, he periodically stopped and let things settle on the horizon.

Most people scanned an area looking for movement, but, in this case, Nikolai was looking for something completely different. It took him a minute, and then he found it. With a smile, he pulled out his phone and sent a message to Mountain, giving him rough coordinates.

Mountain immediately responded. **Hold up. I'm coming.** Making arrangements to reach the new target together, he headed down, and meeting up with Mountain, they both pushed on, anxious to see who and what was hiding just ahead of them.

DAY 4 EVENING

HATING TO BE left behind, but knowing this was how this would go, Emily waited a good forty minutes for Joe to come back. When he didn't, she started to get edgy. In her mind, she had to wonder if he was somehow a part of this. Had he seen what had happened? Did he have any indication of what was going on?

She hated the thoughts running around her head, but she found it hard not to go there, especially when she had nothing to do but sit here and cuddle the dogs. She laughed and played with them and generally took up the equivalent of another hour with them.

Finally she got to her feet and looked down at them. "Maybe I need to go track him down," she muttered to herself, and, before she had a chance to think it through, she was moving. She quickly pulled on her jacket, geared up, and, as she did so, the door opened. and Joe walked in. She looked at him. "Hey, I was coming to look for you."

He chuckled. "Oh, I sat down and had a game of cards with the guys. Haven't done something like that in a while. But, with everybody's attitude being so difficult right now," he added, "it seemed prudent to not say something, or to at least just sit and visit for a bit."

"I'm sure they all appreciated it too," she said, relieved that he was fine. "With so many people going missing, and you not coming back, I was getting worried."

"Didn't realize you were waiting for me," he replied, a question in his tone. "What's going on here?"

"Not a whole lot," she replied, trying to keep the lid on it as long as she could. "Everybody's happily tucked in here against the storm outside."

He nodded. "They're generally a pretty happy lot." He walked over and cuddled a couple of the dogs that had come to meet him.

"They do love you, don't they?"

"Sometimes they love too many people," he replied in a gentle voice, as he cuddled them. He straightened up, and she realized he had a big thermos in his hand. "What's that, dinner or coffee?"

"Coffee," he replied, with a smile. "Nothing like trying to stay warm up here." She nodded. "You go on now, we'll be fine."

"Okay, I just wanted to confirm that you were okay."

"Oh, I'm fine." Joe gave her a wave of his hand. "Go on now. Get lost." Taking that as the dismissal it was, she walked out of the barn area and, bracing against the cold, she walked over to the main area of the compound. When she got there, the guys hanging around the dining room area were playing poker. Relieved that at least that much of Joe's story sounded true, she walked over and made herself a hot cup of tea.

She got a few catcalls but nothing major, which she thought was a good thing. They were rambunctious but not in an ugly way. She quickly walked to the medical clinic, and there she stopped. When she saw Sydney sitting at her desk, doing paperwork, she joined her. "You sure have a lot of paperwork."

She laughed. "Yeah, and sometimes the paperwork is just an excuse." She looked up from her pile of papers. "How are you doing?" she asked Emily.

"I'd be better if Mountain and Nikolai were back," she admitted, assuming that the doc would know that the two men had left, and, from the look on her face, she did.

"You and me both," she said, putting down her pen. She hesitated and asked, "Any problems with anybody?"

Emily shook her head. "Not tonight, or at least not so far. The guys all seem to be happily playing cards in the dining room at the moment."

"Good," Sydney noted. "They were worked a little harder than normal today."

"I'm not against that," Emily agreed, "particularly if it keeps everybody in line."

"We're both on the same page there. Are you heading to bed?"

"Nope. Dinner's still coming, and I'm cold, but I'm not that cold, and I want the guys back safe first."

"Dinner is in progress, or at least it should be out soon." Then Sydney frowned. "I'm not sure why I thought you'd be heading to bed."

"Maybe because I look like hell?" she asked, with a laugh.

"You do look exhausted," the doc noted, with a smile, "and I suspect you didn't get much sleep last night either, did you?"

"No, and I doubt I'll get much tonight either at the rate we're going," she pointed out in a low voice.

"And yet, that's what you need," Sydney said.

Emily snorted. "What I need versus what I'll get? That's a whole different story."

"Sorry. I'm sure the guys will be back soon."

"That's what I was assuming as well, but, since they aren't back yet, in the back of my mind I have to wonder if something else has gone wrong."

"I hope not," Sydney muttered. "Been enough going wrong on this trip to last me a lifetime."

"I know, right? But, for now, I'll remind myself that they are extremely capable men, and I'll head to my room, and that should make life a little easier for me."

And, with that, Sydney started stacking up her papers.

"I'll talk to Nikolai and Mountain whenever they come in," Emily stated, "but I'll come for dinner in another twenty minutes or so, after the crowd has gone through."

"Are you still avoiding people?" Sydney asked, looking at her intently.

"No, I'm not avoiding anybody," she began and then hesitated. "Well, maybe. I don't really want to start anything, but I didn't do anything to start the last scenario, so it's just a matter of playing it smart."

"Why don't you relax here for a few minutes, while I finish up? Then we'll go to dinner together."

Emily hesitated, a little embarrassed. "Are you sure?"

"Sure, I'm sure," Sydney said. "A couple of the other women might join us too."

"Oh, cool, that sounds fun. I haven't seen Berry much."

"Yeah, she's been laying low, recovering still."

"As long as she's okay," Emily noted, with concern.

"She's doing okay. It's just that the psychological mending takes a bit."

"Exactly," Emily muttered. She sat in the other chair and waited quietly for Sydney to finish whatever she was doing, and, when she finally had all the papers in their appropriate files, she locked up the clinic.

"Whew," Sydney muttered. "Glad that's done. Now let's go get some dinner, and hopefully, by the time we're done eating, they'll be back."

"Do we do anything if they aren't?" Emily asked.

"That's not my role, but, if a search party were needed, we certainly are equipped here to handle it. I would hope they'll be back soon, but I also know someone is assigned to keep track of their progress," she shared. "So, if it takes them a little longer, it takes them a little longer."

As they walked into the kitchen, Magnus stood there, off to the side, Samson ever quiet at his side. But that gaze of Magnus's didn't miss much. When he saw the two of them, he walked over with a smile and said to Sydney, "You finally got hungry, did you?"

She chuckled. "More or less."

"Have you heard anything?" Emily asked in a low voice.

He shook his head. "I got a message about an hour ago that they found another campsite, and they were off on the hunt, following tracks."

"Oh, good," Emily said. "That is progress."

"It is, and we've sent out Barret and Egan for backup, though I haven't heard back from them yet."

Sydney nodded, stepped into line, quickly picked up a plate, and got some food. The others followed suit, and, as they all sat down, normal conversations slowly resumed around them.

As they started to eat, Emily looked over at Magnus. "Did Mountain tell you anything before he took off?"

He looked at her curiously and then said that they'd only spoken on the phone for a few minutes, though he'd mentioned he learned a few interesting things over at the dog run.

She smiled with relief. "Well, good, I'm glad he said something to you."

Samson nodded in agreement.

Something was almost familiar about him, but Emily couldn't place him. He stayed in the background. An unnerving shadow that constantly watched but rarely spoke. She'd heard low mutters about the new addition to the investigation team, but, outside of sideways looks, no one mentioned anything directly about his presence.

"You were over there at the dog barn most of the day, weren't you?" Magnus asked Emily.

"Yeah, first half waxing the skis and then the second half waiting to make sure Joe came back."

"He took an early dinner back with him."

She frowned at that. "If he did, it was in soup form in his thermos. Other than that, I didn't see him bring anything over."

He frowned, a bit confused, then added, "Joe was playing cards here for a bit with the guys. He might have eaten while he was here, and he also said something about not having much of an appetite these days."

She lowered her voice. "I think the drinking may be getting worse."

He didn't say anything, just nodded in concern. "I'll keep note of that."

Relieved, but feeling like a tattletale, Emily shut up and quickly finished her dinner. When she was done, she looked around at Sydney and Magnus. "I might as well head back to my room." Then she frowned and added, "First I think I'll head over and check on Joe again."

"Why is that?" Magnus asked, looking at her sharply.

She winced. "I don't have any real reason, just that ... I don't know. Instincts, I guess."

"You have to listen to that," Magnus confirmed. "It's one of the most critical skills we have, but it takes time to learn to read it, and sometimes you're right, and sometimes you're not."

"Meaning, right now I'm likely not, but, hey, you'll humor me."

He laughed. "As I said... we have to interpret those feelings. If it's just worry, learn to separate it out from the instincts, and it'll help you in the long run."

Nodding, she got up, walked over, put up her dishes, and, on second thought, made herself a cup of tea and walked out with it. She glanced around to see who was still here but saw no sign of her tormentors. So, feeling as if the coast was clear, she headed out to the main hallway and then to her room. As she got closer to her room, she heard a whisper behind her.

Wincing, she realized that somehow, they'd come up behind her, but were still hanging back a little bit. She dared not turn around and go back the way she came, but she didn't want to go to her room now either. Thankfully, still some hallways between them, she made a quick turn, then picked up her pace, took a roundabout way, then quickly geared up and slipped out to check on Joe. It had been her instinctive reaction to go there anyway, both to make sure he was all right, and hopefully to see if the guys had returned.

But, at this moment, it also got her away from the assholes who had been following her. She didn't even know for sure that they were following her, but she wanted to avoid a confrontation, and this seemed to be the best answer. As she walked in to check on Joe, he was singing off-tune to the dogs. She laughed when she heard him. He looked and grinned. "Hey, the pretty lady's back again."

"I don't know about *pretty lady*, but I'm definitely back to check up on you and to make sure everything's okay out here."

"I don't know what I did to deserve another visit," Joe replied, "but you are welcome anytime." He sang a few words of welcome, then patted the seat beside him. She sat down near enough that they could talk.

"Tell me. Are you trying to avoid somebody out there?" Joe asked her.

"I am trying to avoid a few people," she admitted, with a smile, "but that's kind of a new development."

He nodded. "In a place like this, it can get pretty ugly sometimes."

"It sure can," she agreed, "and I want to avoid ugly, if that's an option."

"It should always be an option, but it's not necessarily a good one."

She wasn't quite sure what he meant or if he even knew. He went on, rambling more and more about the days when he was in active service. She listened to him talk, happy that he was in a good mood, and content to just be who he was today. She'd never had any problem with him in all the time that she'd been there, and, whenever his ramble came to a stop, she asked a question, just to keep the conversation going. "Will you be happy to go home after this?"

"Yep, I sure will," Joe stated, "and I think it'll be my last trip. This old knee of mine"—he stretched it out in front of her—"isn't very happy."

"No, I'm sure the cold is not very easy on any joints," she muttered, thinking about it. "Cold often affects us that way, doesn't it?"

"Sure does," Joe agreed, with half a smile. "So far, it hasn't been a problem or held me back, but this trip is really starting to wear people down, even me. So, I can read the writing on the wall, as well as the next guy." Joe gave her a knowing smile.

"Only if you're ready," she said. "I know most everybody here appreciates having you."

He laughed at that. "I don't know that anybody appreciates having *me* here," he clarified, smiling ruefully. "The dogs are a welcome distraction, and of course it's part of the training, but, to be honest, most of the people on base would cheerfully do without the dogs."

Surprised, she looked at him. "I don't think that's true."

"That's because you like dogs," Joe pointed out, "but not everybody does. Not everybody here wants the headache of dealing with them, and, when you're out there and you're dealing with them, it's very much a survival thing. That's not everybody's cup of tea either."

She pondered that, even as she wrapped her arms around Bertie again and hugged him close. She loved this damn dog. And, if she could keep him afterward, she would be in heaven. As she cuddled the dog, Joe went off on another ramble of his military days, and, when he finally ran dry again, he patted her arm. "You shouldn't be sitting here, listening to me." He gave a wave of his hand. "I'm sure some young buck is out there who you would much rather visit with."

"Yep, there sure is," she admitted, chuckling, "but he's out tracking right now." Joe frowned at her, and she nodded absentmindedly. "The guys are out hunting some tracks."

"Ah." Joe nodded. "The good ones, the protectors."

"That they are."

"They aren't all like that, you know? I've certainly seen enough in my day that makes me wonder why they're even in the service at all if they don't mean to protect." Joe smiled at her. "Maybe you'll find somebody this trip."

"I'm definitely not looking for somebody," she noted.

"That's the best time to find someone." Joe laughed loudly, and, with that, he launched off into an explanation of how he met his wife. She listened with amusement, realizing he was more boozed up than she'd expected. She wondered how much he was allowed to get away with on a military base, when nobody else was drinking. Yet, as a contractor, Joe might well have more latitude than the rest of them who were on active duty.

She suspected that tonight Joe was likely well past that. What harm was it though? She couldn't imagine, except for the fact that they apparently had somebody utilizing his space as a transportation route and a temporary hideout.

As he was talking, he started to nod off, and she watched in amusement as he slowly drifted off to sleep. Feeling protective and still wanting to keep an eye on the place, she curled up in a bunch of the blankets, while he snored gently nearby.

She must have drifted off herself because, when she heard a sudden noise, she opened her eyes to see somebody, a stranger, come through one of the dog doors. She stared for a moment, thinking it must be Nikolai and Mountain. Yet, as she came fully awake, that was not Nikolai. It was likely the man who everybody was looking for. Yet she had no idea who he was or what he wanted.

He straightened up and slowly looked around, then stiffened when he saw her, still curled up and pretending to be asleep, with Joe snoring at her side. She watched under her lashes, trying not to do anything but appear to be sound asleep. When he took several steps toward her and raised his hand, she noted he had a firearm, and the jig was up. "Who are you, and what are you doing here?" she asked, as she moved to sit up.

Raising the handgun, he thundered, "Don't even move."

She glared at him. "I asked, who are you, and what are you doing here?"

Joe mumbled something beside her, but she willed him back to sleep. Having him sleep through this would be far better than having him awake and drunk in the midst of this mess right now. She frowned at the stranger again. "How in the hell are you even coming and going in this place?"

"It's easy," he said. "I half belong."

"Half belong?" she repeated, not really understanding what he was saying, just knowing that he was trying to pull the wool over her eyes. "I've never seen you before."

"That's because you never fucking looked," he said in disgust. "But then what do you expect?"

She blinked. "Sorry?"

"I came in with the supplies."

"Aren't you supposed to leave with the supplies too?" she asked.

"Supposed to, only last time I didn't," he replied, "and that was something Eric set up."

"Oh, so you're looking for Eric then? I'm so sorry."

"Yeah, so am I because he got me into this mess." The gunman kept both a steady gaze and the gun on her. "Now, I need to get myself out of it."

"Can't you just sneak back out on the next supply run?"

"Wouldn't that be nice? Apparently that's not so easy,"

he replied, "and I don't have the money to bribe the pilot again."

"Maybe you could convince him that the initial bribery was for the trip out as well," she suggested, trying to sound hopeful.

He shook his head at that. "Don't be stupid."

She glared at him. "Look. I don't even know what you're doing here, but, if you had anything to do with the mess that Eric was involved in, trust me. You don't want to be here."

"No, I probably don't," he agreed. "I shouldn't have gotten involved in this shit anyway," he muttered, glaring right back at her. "But now that I am, I have to find a way out of it."

"So, what will you do? Holding a firearm on me isn't exactly encouraging."

"Yeah, well, for all I know, you've got one pointed at me, and I can't see it for the dark."

That's when she realized how nervous he was. "I guess it's been pretty rough living out there without Eric, *huh?*"

He nodded. "Yeah, he's the one who got me caught up in this bullshit," he muttered. "I shouldn't have had anything to do with it."

"If you hadn't had anything to do with it, you would have been a whole lot better off, I'm sure," she stated, "but what is it you're expecting anybody to do for you now?"

"I want to go back," he stated. "I want to go back home and still be breathing when I do it."

"Do you know what Eric was up to?"

"No, he didn't tell me." He glared at her. "What's it to you?"

"I was thinking I might help," she offered, "but I understand you may not want help at this point."

"Yes, I do want some fucking help, but only from somebody who can get me out of here. Someone who can get me stateside and out of this fucking mess."

"I can do that," she stated, staring at him, willing him to stay calm and to not suddenly lose it. At the same time, she needed Joe to stay quiet as well. "Look. I can talk to the people here, and I am sure we can sort this out."

"No, nobody'll sort anything out," he spat. "It's too far gone."

"Why? Did you kill anybody?" she asked. "Because if it's less than that, I don't think anybody will be too worried about it being too far gone. Besides, you've got information they need."

He stared at her and shook his head. "I didn't kill anybody. I swear I didn't, but Eric did."

She winced. "Yeah, I can almost see that," she muttered. "He died attacking a woman here."

He stared at her in shock. "Really?"

"Yes, really," she said, trying to keep the conversation going. "Whether he meant to or not, I don't know, but it's not as if anybody here was prepared to take a chance, when he went off the wall."

"No, no, you don't understand. He told me that … he, he would take care of things, would clean it all up, and would ensure we could both get out of here."

"And yet, in the end, I don't think that was on his mind at all," she countered sympathetically. "At least … not the version I heard of it."

"And, of course, you'll listen to that version, won't you?"

"I'm not sure I'm listening to any version. More to the point, I'm concerned about you standing there, holding a gun on me."

He looked at the weapon in his hand, almost sorrowfully. "It's a hell of a freaking mess right now," he muttered. "I don't even know how to get out of it."

"You get out of it by telling the truth," she stated, "and that means you talk to me."

"I don't know anything about you." He glared at her. "For all I know, you are part of the group that's been hunting me."

"Did you really expect people not to go after you?" she asked. "Think about it. Eric's dead, and it's obvious he's not been working alone. Nobody really has any idea just how in-depth this headache has become, and now here you are, standing here, holding a gun on me. They want answers. That's what they want primarily. Answers."

He shook his head. "I don't have any answers."

"Okay, so Eric arranged for you to get off the cargo plane and paid off the pilot, so he was okay to not report you, is that it?"

He nodded. "That's what Eric did. Did you guys get any alerts that I was missing?"

She shook her head. "No, I never did hear that anybody else was missing. So, good job on Eric's part. You basically disappeared, and nobody knew."

"Something like that," the gunman replied, "but it wasn't supposed to be forever, just for a few days. A few days."

"And then what?" she asked.

"Then he would come back with me, and this would be over with."

"Okay, so he would find you and somehow arrange for you guys to get back onto a plane without being seen," she pointed out, "and then get your life back."

"Exactly. I had holiday time coming, and, according to whatever he'd arranged, I was just gone on a holiday. But now that the time is racking up, and you say Eric's dead, I feel as if I've been shafted in the deal, yet I don't quite understand how."

Honestly he did sound completely bewildered, which made her even more confused. "Do you know why Eric wanted you to stay behind? What was it supposed to be for?"

Then he stopped and suddenly glared at her. "You said a woman killed Eric," he snapped. "Was that you?"

"No, it wasn't me."

He snorted. "It's not as if I can believe you."

"Yes, you can." She stood up.

He waved the gun at her. "Get back. Sit down again."

She hesitated, and he took a step forward. She slowly sat back down and asked calmly, "Why can't you go back out on the next supply run?"

"I would if I could. I already tried."

She shook her head. "We haven't had any supply runs in a few days."

"Eric told me that he couldn't get me out again, that nobody was willing to take a chance."

She winced. "Did you ever think that maybe … he just didn't want you to leave?"

He stared at her. "It doesn't fucking matter now," he snapped, "because Eric's dead, and I'm stuck here in this mess."

"And yet there'll be more supply runs, more planes getting out of here," she pointed out. "You can't survive out there on your own for long."

He stiffened and glared at her.

"I know. I know. That was his thing. He was really good

at it, but are you as good as Eric?"

"I wouldn't be out here if I wasn't."

"So why don't you just tell me what the hell Eric was actually doing?"

"I'm not telling you nothing. All I'm saying is that he wanted help. He was a really good friend of mine, and he needed somebody to help him get vengeance."

She stiffened and nodded. "Okay, I hear that. Do you know Nikolai?"

He sneered. "Yeah, he came to talk to Nikolai, and I need to talk to Nikolai myself," he declared, with a wave of the gun. "Thought I had that down, but then that all went to crap."

"Then why did you knock him out and stash him in the generator room?" When he stared at her, incredulous, she could see that he hadn't a clue what she was talking about. Her heart sank because that meant somebody else was out here. "Look. Why don't I get you some help? We'll get you inside. Have you even eaten today?"

He hesitated and then shook his head. "No." Suddenly his grip was weak on the gun. "I haven't. I didn't eat yesterday either."

"Okay, that's enough now," she declared in a scolding voice. "Let me get you over to the main building, and we'll get you some food, get you warmed up." She noted the chill around his face. "Have you been coming in here to get warm at night?"

He nodded slowly. "Yeah, I want to go fucking home."

"And we'll get you there. I promise."

He looked at her hesitantly. Then the door burst open, and Nikolai and Mountain stepped in. They turned, their gaze assessing the situation immediately, as the stranger held the gun in her direction. Immediately she stepped in between them and said to them all, "Everybody, stop."

Nikolai looked at her, and she shrugged. "I'm fine. He's been living close to base and was brought in by Eric. He's not the one who knocked you out," she said. "Mountain… we need him. He's cold. He's hungry, and he needs debriefing… but he also needs to be safe."

Nikolai immediately nodded, assessing things quickly. "Fine," he told Emily, then he looked at the gunman. "Is that your campsite we found?"

He nodded. "Probably."

"A mile or two from here?"

At that, his eyebrows shot up, and he shook his head. "In that case, it wasn't."

"Somebody else was working with you, right?" Nikolai asked.

"A friend of Eric's," he said in disgust. "The guy's name is Nikolai."

"I've got news for you. I'm Nikolai," Nikolai replied in astonishment. "And I can tell you that I wasn't working with him at all."

He frowned. "No, that's not right. … Eric told me that you were his buddy and that you would help him. Help him get vengeance."

"Vengeance for what? What's this all about?"

"He didn't say, but I knew it was eating at him, and it was big, really big. He wanted to see the end of it. He told me how it had ruined his life a long time ago, and he wouldn't stand for it anymore. He didn't want anybody else's life ruined."

None of this was making any sense to Nikolai or to her. She turned to Mountain, and he looked equally perplexed.

"Can we get him into his bed?" Emily asked. Mountain caught sight of Joe, still snoozing on the side, and she nodded. "I think the poker game was fairly loaded."

He groaned. "Yeah, dry bases are hard to maintain, particularly with these other issues here, so I understand it." He bent down, picked up the older man, carried him over, and laid him on his bed, then covered him up. "Any idea if the dogs need anything tonight?"

"No, they don't," she replied. "They've been fed, and they can come and go as they want," she said, with a nod toward the stranger. "What's your name?" He frowned at her, and she shrugged. "We'll know very quickly anyway," she said, as she turned to Mountain. "He came in on the supply run, and apparently Eric paid a pilot to stay quiet about it."

Mountain stared at her in disbelief, then turned and frowned at the gunman.

He nodded. "I'm Carl. Eric said he couldn't get me back out again because nobody was willing to take a chance."

"But whether Eric asked anybody or not is another story," she noted.

Carl turned and glared at her. "I told you that he was my best friend."

"I know," she confirmed, "but I also know that Nikolai would've considered Eric his best friend too, and that didn't work out so well."

Nikolai stepped forward, and the gunman didn't move. Carl was completely passive, as Nikolai disarmed him. Looking at him, Carl asked, "You're really Nikolai?"

"I am," he confirmed, looking him full in the face. "Are you seriously not the man who knocked me out and stashed me behind the generator to die in the cold?"

Carl shook his head. "No, I didn't do that. I'm the guy waiting for Eric to come back. He roped me into this, and then suddenly I didn't quite understand what was going on. I started having reservations about it all, but he told me that I couldn't get out, no way to get out now. He said he'd spent all the money trying to get me in, and I needed to not desert him." Carl started to tremble.

Emily looked over at Mountain. "We need to get him back inside." He nodded, and, with Nikolai's help, they quickly ushered him back through the cold and into the main section of the base. As he got inside, he started to shake really badly.

"Down to the medical clinic with you," Nikolai said.

"I'll take him with me," Mountain suggested, with a nod. "He's definitely got to see Sydney."

"Who's Sydney?" Carl asked, looking fearful.

"The doctor."

"Oh." He didn't seem to think anything of that. As they all headed to the clinic, she walked over, looped her arm through Nikolai's, and asked in concern, "And you're doing okay?"

He nodded, but his voice was grim when he added, "That just means somebody else is still out there."

"We don't know who it is though, but Carl swears he didn't attack you, and I knew he was telling the truth right away."

"Carl didn't say what this revenge or payback plan was, did he?" Nikolai asked Emily.

"No, just something from a long time ago," she muttered.

Carl was starting to get really cold, really weak. Finally, a strangled sound came out of his mouth, and Mountain scooped him up before he hit the ground, and, at a rapid clip, carried him to Sydney.

Sydney looked up in surprise, saw the stranger, and bolted to her feet. "What the hell?"

"Hypothermia."

"He's hungry too," Emily added, from behind. "He didn't eat today or yesterday. I'm not so sure he's eaten much very recently at all."

Carl, totally incapable of speaking, tried to shake his head.

Sydney ushered everybody out of the way, then looked over at Emily. "Go get a hot broth for him, as quick as you can, and have Chef put some blankets in to warm."

And, with that, Emily dashed to the kitchen and caught Chef Elijah, who was setting things up for the morning. She explained briefly what she needed, and he quickly put a pot on the stove and heated some broth he had in the cooler.

As soon as he had it ready, she carefully carried it toward the clinic in a big, thick mug. As she walked in, she saw Carl bundled up and shivering badly. She looked over at Sydney. "How's he doing?"

She didn't say anything, but she had the blood pressure cuff on Carl's arm, plus was taking his temperature again.

Emily frowned, as she brought the broth over to him. "We have some hot liquids, and we need to get some of it down you," she murmured. "Sydney's got you bundled up, and those heated blankets are coming soon."

A few minutes later, Mountain came charging back in again with the heated blankets, and, with everybody's efforts, Carl finally started to calm down a little bit. He eagerly sipped at the broth, enough that Emily realized he probably hadn't eaten in several days or at least not well enough.

Emily swore under her breath.

He caught the sound of it and looked at her in fear.

"You could have come in earlier, you know."

He shook his head. "I don't belong here," he muttered. "I don't know what's going on, but somebody'll catch hell for all of this."

She looked over at Mountain, and he nodded. "Yep, somebody is." She knew exactly who that would be, but that was the least of their problems right now. Carl needed help, and he needed it in a big way.

Then the clinic door slammed open, and the colonel stepped forward. Immediately everybody stiffened, as he glared at all of them. His gaze turned to Sydney and then to the stranger on the bed. "Who are you? What are you doing here? How dare you hide in my base," he barked. And that was the first she realized that he obviously knew something. Otherwise, no need to even ask that question.

"I came in with the pilot in the supply flight," Carl muttered. "I was supposed to go back out the same way, but Eric arranged for me to stay behind."

The CO glared at him. "Why the hell would you want to do that?"

Surprised at the question, she stayed quiet. Nikolai tugged her a little closer, almost to keep her out of the line of fire. The conversation went back and forth, but Carl wasn't very coherent and barely talking from the cold.

Sydney stepped forward and addressed the CO. "Respectfully, sir, he's not coherent right now. I'll let you know when he's able to better communicate. Right now, I need to get him warm."

He stared at her and stepped back. "You've got a couple hours hour to get him talking. Otherwise I'll be back, and I'll get answers one way or another." And, with that, he was gone again.

Emily let out her breath, then turned toward Mountain. "You might want to do some damage control."

He shook his head. "Not a whole lot anybody'll do about this one. We need answers and fast. The fact of the matter is, Eric wasn't working alone, and we need to know who he's working with."

"I don't know who he's working with," Carl cried out. "I thought him and me. And some Nikolai guy."

"But what were you to do?" Emily asked.

He looked at her, shamefaced. "He wanted somebody to watch his campsite and to watch his back, while he was out hunting."

"Hunting what?"

"People, one person in particular. He wanted to take them out before they hurt anybody else."

"So, you were okay to watch his campsite and to be there for him, so he could go out and kill somebody?" she asked in horror.

He flushed. "It sounds really bad when you put it that way."

"How do you expect anybody to put it?" she asked, staring at him. "You're an accessory to murder, if nothing else here."

He stared at her in horror. "No, I didn't have anything to do with it."

"And yet you were enabling him for whatever reason." Then she stopped and looked at the others. "Oh my God."

"What?" Nikolai asked, frowning at her.

Even Mountain turned to stare at her. "Speak up," he barked. "What?"

"I know why he was brought here." She turned and looked at him. "He would get the blame. He is the patsy."

A dead silence came for a moment, then Nikolai nodded. "Now that," he replied, lost in his own head, "makes the most sense so far."

"What do you mean?" Carl asked, staring at her, his gaze going from one to the other and back again.

"He brought you out here to take the blame for what he would do, but he didn't get to finish his plan before he died. And now you're the one stuck trying to explain everything," she suggested. "So, in a way, his plan is working, even though you had no idea what Eric was doing."

⊕

As far as Nikolai could figure, Emily was bang on with her theory. Carl was starting to settle in. Nikolai stayed in the medical clinic next to the rattled man for the next two hours, as he rambled from one conversation to the next, as the cold numbed his brain and kept him dozing in and out, even as Sydney kept waking him up.

Eventually his vitals returned to normal, and he passed out in an exhausted sleep. Sydney stood here, checking on him once more, and then shook her head. "I think he's out of the worst of it now. We'll have to see on the hypothermia though. His fingers and one toe look sketchy, so it depends if he'll keep them, but I'm hopeful that we caught him in time."

"Good," Nikolai said, from the side of the bed. "I don't think Carl had any idea what the hell Eric was up to."

Sydney looked over at him and nodded. "I think you're right. I think Eric was working his agenda and had set up

Carl to take the fall. And now that he will, he doesn't know what he's taking the blame for, and that's even sadder."

"Yet it's obvious that he doesn't even know anything," Nikolai noted, "so I don't know how much he can be blamed for."

"It doesn't matter, and you know that. He's here, and he's involved, and he was totally okay with whatever vengeance Eric had planned. The question is, who was he planning vengeance on and why? And what can we do to stop this last person who's involved from partaking in it?"

"Do we know that this person is partaking in anything?"

"You guys never did find whoever was using that other campsite, right? Carl said it wasn't his."

"No," Mountain stated, "but I'm heading out now to check."

Sydney grabbed his hand and said, "No way, no how. You need to give it a few hours. We're in the coldest part of the night right now. As soon as dawn cracks, you can go out there again, and this time you'll get farther than you were because you'll already have a good idea where you're going."

"Maybe," he said, taking a step back. "But the bottom line is, we need to find out who the hell has been out there and bring them in too. It's the only way we'll get answers."

"But it does seem that whoever Eric wanted vengeance on is here… on this base," Nikolai noted in frustration. "Eric already got one innocent dude into this, so what are the chances of there being a second one?"

"Maybe, but this one's also pretty damn smart out there, so maybe it's a local, or maybe Eric paid them to watch his back."

"That's the thing. We don't know anything yet," Nikolai argued. "We can't go judging this third guy because he may not have the slightest idea. I firmly think that Carl here was set up to take the fall. That is classic Eric."

"Eric was an asshole," Mountain declared, glaring at Nikolai. "*That* we have already established."

"First," Sydney suggested, "you guys need to go get some sleep."

"What about you?" Mountain asked, turning to look at her.

"This is my clinic, and I'll run it the way I want, sir, and, right now, I want you guys gone. I want you in bed and getting caught up on your sleep." She pointed to Mountain and then to Nikolai. "Before anybody goes out hunting tomorrow, everybody needs to be warm, rested, and fed," the doc declared. "I don't want any more of these hypothermia cases back on my doorstep." She glared at the men. "Now, the both of you, get going."

Surprised and yet immediately turning, the two men headed out to the hallway, and the doc closed the door firmly behind them. Nikolai glanced over at Mountain. "She, uh, she doesn't take no for an answer, does she?"

Mountain laughed. "No, and she's right, as much as I hate to admit it. We've had a couple rough days. So, a little bit of rest and then I'm heading back out."

"That's good," Nikolai agreed, "but why do I get the feeling you know something I don't."

"I don't know anything for sure. I have a better idea though, and I'm not terribly happy about it," Mountain admitted. "I don't know if that person was with them or not, but I've seen some of those tracks before."

At that, Nikolai stiffened and asked, "Who is it?"

He looked at him with a hard glance. "As far as I can tell, one Dr. Amelia Morrison. She is one of the missing scientists. The last of them actually."

"No way she would help Eric or his cohorts, would she? I mean, why would she?"

"I don't think she was helping him, though she might have been a step ahead of him. It could very well be that he was trying to implicate her in his shenanigans as well, and she knew that she could get caught up in it if anybody ever found her. So, maybe she was just staying the hell away from all this, including us, for that same reason."

"Well, damn," Nikolai muttered, shaken by this suggestion since he hadn't seen that coming. "Weren't those other tracks heading toward the village?"

"Yep, and believe me. I'll be on the village's doorstep at dawn." He looked at his watch and winced. "Okay, so maybe not dawn," he corrected, "but I won't be far behind, and, no, you're not coming with me. Not for this one."

"Why not?" Nikolai asked.

"You know why. The locals don't trust easily. Like it or not, they're used to me, so I'll figure this out and get back," he shared. "Still, I'm pretty-damn sure that Amelia didn't have anything to do with Eric."

"But you can't be 100 percent sure."

"No, I can't," he replied, "but her being involved? … I can't wrap my head around that one. What we need to know is who the hell is here, who somebody wants to kill, and why?"

"You need to talk to the colonel too."

"Not me. Ted and Samson can do that. Now, let's go get some shut-eye."

As they headed down the main hallway, Mountain veered off and headed for his quarters. Heading to his room, Nikolai soon found himself standing outside of Emily's door instead of his own. He groaned, but the door opened right in front of him, and she said cheerfully, "I was hoping you would come."

"I didn't plan on it, but my feet apparently have a mind of their own."

"Isn't that a good thing," she quipped, with a smirk. "Don't just stand there. Come on in." He stepped inside, and, in a firm voice, she immediately added, "Now get into bed and crash."

He looked at her, surprised, but she put up her hand. "No way, don't even start. Come on. You're too tired. You're beyond tired." She quickly helped him undress, aware that he was almost shivering, then she tucked him into bed and curled up tightly against him, her arms wrapped around him.

He groaned. "You're killing me. … Any other day, I would—"

"Any other day you can try it all you want," she murmured, "but right now, you need to sleep."

Closing his eyes, he was asleep within a matter of moments.

DAY 5 EARLY MORNING

EMILY WOKE, SOME furnace wrapped around her, which she'd come to associate with Nikolai. She rolled over to see him staring down at her, a warm twinkle in his gaze. "Hey," she said. "How are you feeling?"

"A hell of a lot better than I was," he murmured. He pulled her up close against him, and she felt the hard ridge between them.

She chuckled. "At least a part of you is awake."

He nodded. "Yeah, and has been for a while, but I didn't want to wake you."

"I appreciate that," she said. "It's been a couple rough days."

"God, has it ever," he agreed, as his head landed back on the pillow. "I didn't expect that to go quite the way it did last night."

"You went after another campsite, didn't you?"

"Yes, and I'll be heading out to the first campsite today to analyze everything we possibly can."

"Good," she replied, shifting her body to rest her face on his bicep. "What about the second campsite and those tracks?"

"Mountain has a pretty good idea what they were, and he's going after them." Nikolai then checked his watch and shot upright in bed. "Damn, I wouldn't be at all surprised if he isn't already gone."

"He might have gone already, but that doesn't mean you have to go anywhere so soon."

"No, but I should be getting up and helping."

She immediately looped her arms around his neck and pulled him back down, so he was lying on top of her. He buried his face against her neck, breathing hot air against her delicate skin. She shivered in reaction. "That feels nice so far, don't you think?"

He lifted his head gently, his tongue and lips working their way across her collarbone, up her neck, and across her jaw. By the time he reached her lips, she was shivering in his arms already, so damn hungry for him that she could hardly think. As soon as his head rose high enough, she pulled him closer for a kiss, a deep but slow warring of tongues, as if a careful mating of emotions and physical wants, as she held him in her arms, feeling her body respond to his restless urging.

He lifted his head to look at her face. "This isn't exactly how I thought we would come together."

"No thinking required at this point," she murmured, with a smile. "I think we're well past that." Shifting her thighs wider, she wrapped them around his hips and started gently rubbing back and forth, pressing upward against him.

⊕

HE SUCKED IN his breath, lowered his head, and closed his eyes.

She whispered, "It would be nice if you didn't hold back right now."

"I don't want it to end so soon," he murmured.

"I'm not worried at all about it ending so soon because I fully expect to be back here again."

He chuckled. "God, I hope so," he replied fervently, as he shifted to be at the heart of her. But it was all he could do to hold back, clenching his jaw as he fought for control, and he whispered. "This time …"

She placed a finger against his lips. "Got it, but next time will be a whole different story."

"I'll have to leave to see where Mountain is."

"Yeah, I know, and I need to get up too," she noted, "but right now it's our time." He started to move inside her, and she exploded almost instantly beneath him, her cries slipping out. He quickly sealed her mouth with his and cuddled her close. Then he started to move again and again, and, by his fourth and then fifth drive, he came apart in her arms, her mouth silencing his cries.

When he collapsed beside her, he groaned. "You damn-near killed me."

"Trying to keep quiet damn-near killed both of us," she whispered, with a giggle.

He looked at her and grinned. "I know, right?" He rolled over and pulled her into his arms. "I really don't want to get up and leave you just yet."

"No, and I don't either, but considering how much of the mystery might get broken apart today, you don't want to miss it." She gave him a kiss on the jaw. "So I don't have a problem getting up and sorting this out."

"No, you're right." He pushed back the covers and almost immediately winced at the cold that connected with his body, sending a shiver down his spine. "How about a holiday in California when this is over?"

"I live in California, so how about you come for a visit?"

He nodded.

"That could work, unless you end up with responsibilities in Switzerland or Germany after this."

"I don't know where I'm going," he said. "I'll touch base with my family, but then I can always come visit you, assuming I get an invitation."

"Consider yourself invited," she said, with a smile. "By the time we figure out where and what we're after in this lovely winter wonderland, we should be doing pretty well, as relationships go."

"Yeah, it'll take us a day or two to sort it out."

"We've got a good start, and I'm not going anywhere. And, if it's up to me, neither are you."

He laughed. "I'm really glad you feel that way."

"Oh, I'm definitely feeling that way," she confirmed.

"Does that mean you're getting dressed now?"

"I am." She groaned but quickly slipped on her clothes, and, giggling now, the two of them ran to their respective bathrooms down the hall for a quick wash up. When she stepped out, he stood there waiting for her.

He grinned. "I figured we should check in at the clinic first and then head to get coffee."

"Okay," she said, "although coffee is always my preferred first choice."

"It's kind of on the way though," he pointed out.

"True."

As they headed to the medical clinic, Sydney stepped out from her room next door. She looked back at them, smiled, and, in a pleasant morning tone, asked him, "Hey. How are you doing?"

"I'm fine," Nikolai replied, "How's our patient?"

"He's good. I popped over to my room to change

clothes. He was doing fine." She walked over, opened the clinic door, and stepped in. Immediately she cried out. They piled into the room behind her and there, half off the bed, was Carl, and obviously he was dead.

※

Nikolai pulled Emily close, as they stared at the dead man.

"Damn it," she whispered. "I told him that I would help him get home." She wrapped her arms around Nikolai.

"I know," he muttered, then turned to Sydney, who was crouched beside her dead patient. "Was anybody here when you left?"

She shook her head. "No, and not only was nobody here when I left, he was awake." The doc sounded weary, as if her voice was coming from very far away. "He had come to a place where he was quite happy to open up and to tell what he knew, though he said he didn't have much more than what he'd told us already."

"What did you talk about? Was there anything new?"

"I told him a supply flight was coming in today. I didn't promise, of course, since I'm not the CO around here, but I planned to make a pitch to the colonel to see about sending Carl out on today's run. Still in custody, of course, but I wanted to get him to a hospital that stood a better chance of saving his fingers. He got really excited. I popped out for a minute to wash and to get changed out of yesterday's clothes," she explained. "I wasn't gone but maybe ten minutes, tops."

"The question is, did somebody come here and help him out, or did he do this to himself?" Nikolai asked.

Magnus stepped into the clinic behind Sydney, his arms wrapping around her and holding her close, as he stared at the dead man. "Jesus Christ. Somehow, we have to put a stop to this shit."

"I don't know what happened," Sydney muttered, bewildered. "I literally was gone ten minutes, likely even less." She shook her head. "Honest to God, he was fine. He was talking. He was okay."

"But this"—Magnus pointed to the dead body, with its blueish sheen on his lips—"looks as if he was poisoned."

"Absolutely." Sydney stared at the dead man. "What I don't know is whether he killed himself the minute he got an opportunity, since I've been here the entire night, or, if in that eight-to-ten-minute window, somebody was waiting for that chance and slipped in, taking care of the job themselves."

"We'll find out," Magnus said quietly, as he held her close. He looked back at Nikolai and Emily. "Are you guys doing okay?"

Emily gave him a lackluster nod. "We're okay, but I've got to tell you. The holiday in California we were just talking about is sounding better all the time. I can't wait to get out of here."

He gave her a warm smile. "Yeah, Sydney and I feel the same way right about now. This has been the trip from hell, though, until I walked in just now, I had hopes that we were getting to the bottom of it."

Nikolai then spoke up. "We are. Either way, this was the act of a desperate man," he noted. "Although Emily and I have got our present sorted—and at least the next few steps of our future planned for," he added, "we still have the last few things here to tie up."

At that, Magnus looked at him. "So, does that mean you have a good idea of what's going on?"

"Let me put it this way. I have a hell of a lot better idea than I did last night," he declared, as he stared at the dead man.

Magnus nodded. "Now we have to consider that fact that everybody in this compound had a chance to kill Carl and, as such, are all murder suspects."

"Unless he took the poison on his own," Sydney repeated, turning toward him.

"How did he get the poison? Did he have access to poison?"

"The medicine cabinet is still locked, and I don't have any drugs anywhere else."

"So, somebody else had access to poison, and that is as big a deal as anything." Magnus shook his head.

Nikolai added, "And it may be that somebody came in here and convinced Carl that he needed to take it, but chances are, he didn't even have that long to consider it." Nikolai sighed. "As far as I'm concerned, this man was murdered, and now we need Mountain to return to bring in the final pieces to this puzzle."

"I don't know about final pieces," Sydney noted, staring at him in shock. "But, damn, I hope you're right because I need this to come to an end."

"It'll come to an end, all right," Nikolai agreed, with a nod, "but now we've all got paperwork to do and more research to work on. And hopefully, if Mountain brings back the right answers, we should get this sorted real fast."

Then came a shout from the far end of the hallway, and Mountain strode toward them, another man in his arms.

Sydney stared at him. "Oh my God, another one? Who

is this now?" Sydney cried out.

Mountain gave her a half smile, and his expression revealed all kinds of emotions, as his panting wouldn't get words out.

Emily took one look at the battered face of the man, and her heart did a flip in her chest, and she squeezed Nikolai's arm.

"Sydney, it's Teegan. Teegan Rode."

EPILOGUE

TEEGAN OPENED HIS eyes, only to slam them shut against the bright light. He moaned ever-so-softly as pain shivered through him. Gentle hands put a warm cloth against his forehead and gently wiped his face. "What happened?" he whispered.

"That'll be one of the questions I ask of you," a woman replied.

He opened his eyes to see a man standing there, looking ferocious, and a woman beside him, gently wiping his face.

"Who are you?" he whispered.

"I'm Sydney. I'm the doctor here. I arrived not long after you disappeared."

He blinked at her several times and asked, "Where?"

At that, Mountain stepped forward. "Teegan, do you know who I am?"

He nodded. "Yeah, you're the guardian angel I've been praying for."

"Yeah, I'm here, brother. I'm just so damn sorry it took me so long to find you."

"I'm alive. That's what counts," he muttered, "but I sure as hell wish you could tell me what the hell happened."

"We'll get there. I'm not sure how much you remember or how much you'll ever remember," Mountain said, "but you're here now, and we'll protect you. You are the reason I came up here."

"Thank you for that," he added, as he opened his eyes. "Did you save the woman?"

"What woman?" Mountain asked, stepping forward.

"The one who was helping me."

"Was it Amelia?"

"Yes, Amelia."

"Why does she need saving?" Mountain asked, his voice choking up.

"She's the one who kept me alive. She's the one who kept moving me around to keep me alive," he shared, and then he winced. "Damn, it's really hard to keep a hold on the memories. Everything keeps shifting and mixing together."

At Teegan's side, Sydney turned to Mountain. "You'll need to give him a chance to rest and to get his thoughts together," she stated. "Everything'll be hazy, and, once again, we're dealing with the effects of that debilitating cold."

Mountain nodded. "I'll go get him a hot cup of tea."

At that, Teegan opened his eyes and stared at his brother. With a groan and a note of amusement in his voice, he said, "Tea? Really, bro? I would kill for a coffee just now."

Mountain looked over at Sydney, and she nodded. "Get him a coffee," she replied. "The stimulant won't hurt him at this point in time, and it might even help."

At that, Teegan whispered, "Christ, if only I could get warm."

"We'll get you warm," the doc declared, "but I see frostbite on your toes."

He nodded. "Yeah, I don't remember how or where."

Mountain glanced to the other bed. "And, Jesus Christ, somebody needs to fill me in on what the hell happened to

Carl."

Teegan looked over at Mountain. "You need to find Amelia."

"I'll find her," Mountain promised, "but we need to sort you out first."

Then a knock came on the clinic door, and another woman stepped in. She looked over at Sydney. "Doctor? I'm Sandrine," she stated. "I came in on the supply plane. I understand you've been a little overwhelmed."

"Yeah, you could say that," Sydney admitted. "I had somebody helping, but she's been quite sick."

"I'm not, and I'm here and ready to help wherever I can." She walked over to Teegan, then looked at him and winced. "Teegan?"

He raised heavy eyelids and stared at her in confusion. "Sorry, do I know you?"

Disappointment crossed her face, and then she shrugged. She looked over at Sydney and masked her features in an instant. "What can I do to help?"

Immediately noticing the unmistakable hurt in her voice, Sydney smiled at her. "Teegan's come back from an extremely rough ordeal, and we don't know the details yet," she explained. "Unfortunately neither does he. His memories aren't there, and he doesn't have any recollection of what's happened to him. Please don't take offense to anything he says right now."

Sandrine looked at her in shock.

Teegan opened his eyes. "I still don't remember you, but the doc's right. Everything is hazy, and I'm far from 100 percent. Sorry, I'm not trying to insult you."

"That's fine," she replied gently, as she looked at him. "I won't take it personally then."

"I gather I know you?"

"You could say so," she stated. "At one point in time, you asked me to marry you."

This concludes Book 6 of Shadow Recon: Nikolai.
Read about Nikolai: Shadow Recon, Book 7

Shadow Recon: Teegan (Book #7)

Deep in the permafrost of the Arctic, a joint task force, comprised of over one dozen countries, comes together to level up their winter skills. A mix of personalities, nationalities, and egos bring out the best—and the worst—as these globally elite men and women work and play together. They rub elbows with hardy locals and a group of scientists gathered close by …

One fatality is almost expected with this training. A second is tough but not a surprise. However, when a third goes missing? It's hard to not be suspicious. When the missing man is connected to one of the elite Maverick team members and is a special friend of Lieutenant Commander Mason Callister? All hell breaks loose …

Battered and bruised, Teegan wakes up in the training camp struggling to remember the details of his last few weeks. But along with not knowing what happened to him, he also doesn't recognize the woman caring for him back in the camp. According to this Sandrine, he'd once asked her to marry him. Yet, he has no idea who she is…He didn't remember much about what happened, nor did he remember the woman looking after him. Sandrine that is. That information rolls through his confused brain along with the other disjointed bits of information he can't place, leaving him distrustful of everyone around him.

Sandrine can't believe the injured sick man in front of her is Teegan. They had a history together but she'd not in any way thought she'd see him like this. He'd always been so fit and strong. All she wants is to get him back on his feet and be the man she used to know. But someone isn't done with him yet…

Teegan knows his brother is doing everything possible to solve these mysteries and to make sure no one gets a second chance to hurt him. But sometimes betrayal doesn't come from the outside… sometimes it comes from the inside… inside… and not outside…

Find Book 7 here!
To find out more visit Dale Mayer's website.
https://geni.us/DMSSRTeegan

Author's Note

Thank you for reading Nikolai: Shadow Recon, Book 6! If you enjoyed the book, please take a moment and leave a short review.

Dear reader,

I love to hear from readers, and you can contact me at my website: www.dalemayer.com or at my Facebook author page. To be informed of new releases and special offers, sign up for my newsletter or follow me on BookBub. And if you are interested in joining Dale Mayer's Reader Group, here is the Facebook sign up page.
http://geni.us/DaleMayerFBGroup

Cheers,
Dale Mayer

About the Author

Dale Mayer is a *USA Today* best-selling author, best known for her SEALs military romances, her Psychic Visions series, and her Lovely Lethal Garden cozy series. Her contemporary romances are raw and full of passion and emotion (Broken But … Mending, Hathaway House series). Her thrillers will keep you guessing (Kate Morgan, By Death series), and her romantic comedies will keep you giggling (*It's a Dog's Life*, a stand-alone novella; and the Broken Protocols series, starring Charming Marvin, the cat).

Dale honors the stories that come to her—and some of them are crazy, break all the rules and cross multiple genres!

To go with her fiction, she also writes nonfiction in many different fields, with books available on résumé writing, companion gardening, and the US mortgage system. All her books are available in print and ebook format.

Connect with Dale Mayer Online

Dale's Website – www.dalemayer.com
Twitter – @DaleMayer
Facebook Page – geni.us/DaleMayerFBFanPage
Facebook Group – geni.us/DaleMayerFBGroup
BookBub – geni.us/DaleMayerBookbub
Instagram – geni.us/DaleMayerInstagram
Goodreads – geni.us/DaleMayerGoodreads
Newsletter – geni.us/DaleNews

Also by Dale Mayer

Published Adult Books:

Shadow Recon
Magnus, Book 1
Rogan, Book 2
Egan, Book 3
Barret, Book 4
Whalen, Book 5
Nikolai, Book 6
Teegan, Book 7

Bullard's Battle
Ryland's Reach, Book 1
Cain's Cross, Book 2
Eton's Escape, Book 3
Garret's Gambit, Book 4
Kano's Keep, Book 5
Fallon's Flaw, Book 6
Quinn's Quest, Book 7
Bullard's Beauty, Book 8
Bullard's Best, Book 9
Bullard's Battle, Books 1–2
Bullard's Battle, Books 3–4
Bullard's Battle, Books 5–6
Bullard's Battle, Books 7–8

Terkel's Team
Damon's Deal, Book 1
Wade's War, Book 2
Gage's Goal, Book 3
Calum's Contact, Book 4
Rick's Road, Book 5
Scott's Summit, Book 6
Brody's Beast, Book 7
Terkel's Twist, Book 8
Terkel's Triumph, Book 9

Terk's Guardians
Radar, Book 1
Legend, Book 2
Bojan, Book 3
Langdon, Book 4

Kate Morgan
Simon Says… Hide, Book 1
Simon Says… Jump, Book 2
Simon Says… Ride, Book 3
Simon Says… Scream, Book 4
Simon Says… Run, Book 5
Simon Says… Walk, Book 6
Simon Says… Forgive, Book 7
Simon Says… Swim, Book 8

Hathaway House
Aaron, Book 1
Brock, Book 2
Cole, Book 3
Denton, Book 4

Elliot, Book 5
Finn, Book 6
Gregory, Book 7
Heath, Book 8
Iain, Book 9
Jaden, Book 10
Keith, Book 11
Lance, Book 12
Melissa, Book 13
Nash, Book 14
Owen, Book 15
Percy, Book 16
Quinton, Book 17
Ryatt, Book 18
Spencer, Book 19
Timothy, Book 20
Urban, Book 21
Victor, Book 22
Hathaway House, Books 1–3
Hathaway House, Books 4–6
Hathaway House, Books 7–9

The K9 Files
Ethan, Book 1
Pierce, Book 2
Zane, Book 3
Blaze, Book 4
Lucas, Book 5
Parker, Book 6
Carter, Book 7
Weston, Book 8
Greyson, Book 9

Rowan, Book 10
Caleb, Book 11
Kurt, Book 12
Tucker, Book 13
Harley, Book 14
Kyron, Book 15
Jenner, Book 16
Rhys, Book 17
Landon, Book 18
Harper, Book 19
Kascius, Book 20
Declan, Book 21
Bauer, Book 22
Delta, Book 23
The K9 Files, Books 1–2
The K9 Files, Books 3–4
The K9 Files, Books 5–6
The K9 Files, Books 7–8
The K9 Files, Books 9–10
The K9 Files, Books 11–12

Lovely Lethal Gardens
Arsenic in the Azaleas, Book 1
Bones in the Begonias, Book 2
Corpse in the Carnations, Book 3
Daggers in the Dahlias, Book 4
Evidence in the Echinacea, Book 5
Footprints in the Ferns, Book 6
Gun in the Gardenias, Book 7
Handcuffs in the Heather, Book 8
Ice Pick in the Ivy, Book 9
Jewels in the Juniper, Book 10

Killer in the Kiwis, Book 11
Lifeless in the Lilies, Book 12
Murder in the Marigolds, Book 13
Nabbed in the Nasturtiums, Book 14
Offed in the Orchids, Book 15
Poison in the Pansies, Book 16
Quarry in the Quince, Book 17
Revenge in the Roses, Book 18
Silenced in the Sunflowers, Book 19
Toes up in the Tulips, Book 20
Uzi in the Urn, Book 21
Victim in the Violets, Book 22
Whispers in the Wisteria, Book 23
X'd in the Xeriscape, Book 24
Lovely Lethal Gardens, Books 1–2
Lovely Lethal Gardens, Books 3–4
Lovely Lethal Gardens, Books 5–6
Lovely Lethal Gardens, Books 7–8
Lovely Lethal Gardens, Books 9–10

Psychic Visions Series
Tuesday's Child
Hide 'n Go Seek
Maddy's Floor
Garden of Sorrow
Knock Knock...
Rare Find
Eyes to the Soul
Now You See Her
Shattered
Into the Abyss
Seeds of Malice

Eye of the Falcon
Itsy-Bitsy Spider
Unmasked
Deep Beneath
From the Ashes
Stroke of Death
Ice Maiden
Snap, Crackle...
What If...
Talking Bones
String of Tears
Inked Forever
Insanity
Psychic Visions Books 1–3
Psychic Visions Books 4–6
Psychic Visions Books 7–9

By Death Series
Touched by Death
Haunted by Death
Chilled by Death
By Death Books 1–3

Broken Protocols – Romantic Comedy Series
Cat's Meow
Cat's Pajamas
Cat's Cradle
Cat's Claus
Broken Protocols 1-4

Broken and... Mending
Skin

Scars
Scales (of Justice)
Broken but… Mending 1-3

Glory
Genesis
Tori
Celeste
Glory Trilogy

Biker Blues
Morgan: Biker Blues, Volume 1
Cash: Biker Blues, Volume 2

SEALs of Honor
Mason: SEALs of Honor, Book 1
Hawk: SEALs of Honor, Book 2
Dane: SEALs of Honor, Book 3
Swede: SEALs of Honor, Book 4
Shadow: SEALs of Honor, Book 5
Cooper: SEALs of Honor, Book 6
Markus: SEALs of Honor, Book 7
Evan: SEALs of Honor, Book 8
Mason's Wish: SEALs of Honor, Book 9
Chase: SEALs of Honor, Book 10
Brett: SEALs of Honor, Book 11
Devlin: SEALs of Honor, Book 12
Easton: SEALs of Honor, Book 13
Ryder: SEALs of Honor, Book 14
Macklin: SEALs of Honor, Book 15
Corey: SEALs of Honor, Book 16
Warrick: SEALs of Honor, Book 17

Tanner: SEALs of Honor, Book 18
Jackson: SEALs of Honor, Book 19
Kanen: SEALs of Honor, Book 20
Nelson: SEALs of Honor, Book 21
Taylor: SEALs of Honor, Book 22
Colton: SEALs of Honor, Book 23
Troy: SEALs of Honor, Book 24
Axel: SEALs of Honor, Book 25
Baylor: SEALs of Honor, Book 26
Hudson: SEALs of Honor, Book 27
Lachlan: SEALs of Honor, Book 28
Paxton: SEALs of Honor, Book 29
Bronson: SEALs of Honor, Book 30
Hale: SEALs of Honor, Book 31
SEALs of Honor, Books 1–3
SEALs of Honor, Books 4–6
SEALs of Honor, Books 7–10
SEALs of Honor, Books 11–13
SEALs of Honor, Books 14–16
SEALs of Honor, Books 17–19
SEALs of Honor, Books 20–22
SEALs of Honor, Books 23–25

Heroes for Hire
Levi's Legend: Heroes for Hire, Book 1
Stone's Surrender: Heroes for Hire, Book 2
Merk's Mistake: Heroes for Hire, Book 3
Rhodes's Reward: Heroes for Hire, Book 4
Flynn's Firecracker: Heroes for Hire, Book 5
Logan's Light: Heroes for Hire, Book 6
Harrison's Heart: Heroes for Hire, Book 7
Saul's Sweetheart: Heroes for Hire, Book 8

Dakota's Delight: Heroes for Hire, Book 9
Tyson's Treasure: Heroes for Hire, Book 10
Jace's Jewel: Heroes for Hire, Book 11
Rory's Rose: Heroes for Hire, Book 12
Brandon's Bliss: Heroes for Hire, Book 13
Liam's Lily: Heroes for Hire, Book 14
North's Nikki: Heroes for Hire, Book 15
Anders's Angel: Heroes for Hire, Book 16
Reyes's Raina: Heroes for Hire, Book 17
Dezi's Diamond: Heroes for Hire, Book 18
Vince's Vixen: Heroes for Hire, Book 19
Ice's Icing: Heroes for Hire, Book 20
Johan's Joy: Heroes for Hire, Book 21
Galen's Gemma: Heroes for Hire, Book 22
Zack's Zest: Heroes for Hire, Book 23
Bonaparte's Belle: Heroes for Hire, Book 24
Noah's Nemesis: Heroes for Hire, Book 25
Tomas's Trials: Heroes for Hire, Book 26
Carson's Choice: Heroes for Hire, Book 27
Dante's Decision: Heroes for Hire, Book 28
Steven's Solace: Heroes for Hire, Book 29
Heroes for Hire, Books 1–3
Heroes for Hire, Books 4–6
Heroes for Hire, Books 7–9
Heroes for Hire, Books 10–12
Heroes for Hire, Books 13–15
Heroes for Hire, Books 16–18
Heroes for Hire, Books 19–21
Heroes for Hire, Books 22–24

SEALs of Steel
Badger: SEALs of Steel, Book 1

Erick: SEALs of Steel, Book 2
Cade: SEALs of Steel, Book 3
Talon: SEALs of Steel, Book 4
Laszlo: SEALs of Steel, Book 5
Geir: SEALs of Steel, Book 6
Jager: SEALs of Steel, Book 7
The Final Reveal: SEALs of Steel, Book 8
SEALs of Steel, Books 1–4
SEALs of Steel, Books 5–8
SEALs of Steel, Books 1–8

The Mavericks
Kerrick, Book 1
Griffin, Book 2
Jax, Book 3
Beau, Book 4
Asher, Book 5
Ryker, Book 6
Miles, Book 7
Nico, Book 8
Keane, Book 9
Lennox, Book 10
Gavin, Book 11
Shane, Book 12
Diesel, Book 13
Jerricho, Book 14
Killian, Book 15
Hatch, Book 16
Corbin, Book 17
Aiden, Book 18
The Mavericks, Books 1–2
The Mavericks, Books 3–4

The Mavericks, Books 5–6
The Mavericks, Books 7–8
The Mavericks, Books 9–10
The Mavericks, Books 11–12

Standalone Novellas
It's a Dog's Life
Riana's Revenge
Second Chances

Published Young Adult Books:

Family Blood Ties Series
Vampire in Denial
Vampire in Distress
Vampire in Design
Vampire in Deceit
Vampire in Defiance
Vampire in Conflict
Vampire in Chaos
Vampire in Crisis
Vampire in Control
Vampire in Charge
Family Blood Ties Set 1–3
Family Blood Ties Set 1–5
Family Blood Ties Set 4–6
Family Blood Ties Set 7–9
Sian's Solution, A Family Blood Ties Series Prequel Novelette

Design series
Dangerous Designs

Deadly Designs
Darkest Designs
Design Series Trilogy

Standalone
In Cassie's Corner
Gem Stone (a Gemma Stone Mystery)
Time Thieves

Published Non-Fiction Books:

Career Essentials
Career Essentials: The Résumé
Career Essentials: The Cover Letter
Career Essentials: The Interview
Career Essentials: 3 in 1

Manufactured by Amazon.ca
Acheson, AB